The Private Notebooks of Katie Roberts

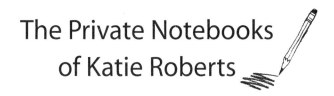

AMY HEST

ILLUSTRATED BY **SONJA LAMUT**

CANDLEWICK PRESS
CAMBRIDGE, MASSACHUSETTS

The Private
Notebook of
Katie Roberts,
age 11

Dear Kate,
This one's for you.
Love,
me,
Mommy
♡

The war came and took my father forever. I was seven.

Weeks passed. I went to school and the library. Months slid into years. I went to temple with my mother, and bought flowers at the market. Oddly, I could still smile. From time to time, I could even laugh. But always, the question: Why did my father die in the war? Why couldn't he just come home, the way you're supposed to?

More upheaval when I was eleven. That was the year Mama decided to marry Sam Gold. We would pack our bags and our lives and move to Sam's ranch in faraway Texas. My mother danced through the rooms, happy again. But I was scared.

My favorite neighbor, Mrs. Leitstein, came to the station to see us off. She was old like a grandmother, cozy and wise. We held hands in the station but did not talk much. There were pearls wrapped in cotton for Mama, all the more precious because they were Mrs. Leitstein's pearls. And for me, a notebook of my own, beautiful red leather with 100 lined pages. You could use the crispy paper to write letters. Or, you could make it private and write anything you wanted. I did both.

Hello, Notebook! It's me, Katie Roberts, age 11. From now on, I am going to write down every single thing that happens. Or at least everything important. And remember, this notebook is **PRIVATE!** No one is allowed to see what's inside, and ESPECIALLY NOT MY MOTHER, who is getting married today at noon. (The man she is getting married to is called Sam Gold. I will maybe tell you more about him later, but first I have to talk about me.)

I am sitting on my new bed in my new room in Texas. There's a canopy, which I like. But I miss my old bed in my old room in New York City and . . . I WISH WE NEVER MOVED HERE 8 DAYS AGO. Why? Because I HATE living on a ranch in the middle of nowhere! It is hot here every minute and this house is too big. There are no neighbors nearby. No subways. Not a single tall building. I LIKE CITIES NOT WILDERNESS, AND I AM NO PIONEER!

Mama says new things take getting used to, but she is wrong. Because I will never get used to Texas and I want to go home now.

And one more thing. I don't understand why SHE (my mother) has to get married all of a sudden. We were fine, just the two of us. Perfectly, wonderfully fine. Now everything is spoiled and it's not fair. Well at least I have new shoes for the wedding. Patent leather with a strap across. They look sensational and gorgeous with pink pajamas, which I am wearing right now. Presenting . . . Katie Roberts tap-dancing pajama queen! I like new shoes. And also pink pajamas.

Katie's Shoes (gorgeous!)

More later. After the w_____.

August 7, 6:00 P.M.

❀ Here I am at Mama's wedding. Miss America, HA! My dress has smocking at the waist and tiny rosebuds all over. ❀

I look very pretty.

Mama did not wear a white dress. She wore navy blue. When I get married, I will only wear white and my dress will be a gown. My mother has a new name, which is Mrs.

3

Sam Gold. She has a new ring, too. It's not that pretty. I like the old one better. My father gave it to her.

We had to drive 30 miles just to find a Texas rabbi, and guess what, he had no beard! I've never seen a rabbi without a beard. This one looked like a regular man and his house was a regular man's house. His wife had red hair, green shoes, and a boy baby called Charlie on her hip. He kept on waving and I waved back. I like babies. When I grow up, I will have a lot. Are you ready for this? THE CEREMONY WAS IN THE KITCHEN! Mama held my hand the whole time and I held hers tight. My stomach was knots. At the end Sam stomped on a glass, which is what you do at a wedding when everyone is Jewish. We all clapped. Even baby Charlie. I was laughing and crying at the same time. Mama, too. Then the groom kissed the bride and she maybe kissed him back. Her hat fell off. I hope that's the end of kissing.

I like weddings and also wedding cake. Especially the kind with whipped cream, and strawberries piled high.

Sam Gold is nice but I wish my father didn't die in the war. I wish he just came home, the way you're supposed to.

Good Cake!

August 14, 4:10 P.M.

Hello again, Notebook! It's me, Katie Roberts, age 11, and I am still in Texas. Mama and Sam the man she married did not go on a honeymoon, but THEY ARE BEHAVING VERY BADLY. They give each other looks and smiles that make me feel left out. I pretend not to notice. I pretend not to care, but I do. For example whenever we drive to town in Sam's old car, they make me sit in back. Dust blows in the window in my mouth and my nose. It isn't fair because THEY sit up front where I can't hear all the things they are saying. Sometimes they sing. The songs they sing are really bad. I like to plug my ears.

Sam took us to the town pool this afternoon. The water is ice! Everyone who goes there knows everyone else. Except me. I don't care, they all look stupid. I swam in the deep end. I went off the high board. There she goes . . . Katie Roberts movie-star champion swimmer! I bet everyone noticed the too-tall girl in a green bathing suit. I bet they are DYING to meet me, ha!

Cows. All you see around here are cows, and also a lot of brownish-greenish grass. Sam used to live in New York like us. But after the war he got this BAD idea to build this dumb old ranch in dumb old Langley. So here I am, stuck for life in the most boring place in the history of the world AND I HATE IT. There is nothing to do in Texas, and no one to do it with, either!

I NEED A BEST FRIEND.

Someone like me with streaky blond hair like my hair sounds nice. We do everything together such as swim at the town pool. We jump in the deep end holding hands and I can teach her how to dive. We laugh all day and tell secrets and lie in the sun on a towel that we share.

I NEED A BEST FRIEND.

NOW!

August 28, 5:02 P.M.

SCHOOL STARTS NEXT MONDAY – **HELP!**
I hope I get sick. Not too sick, just a sore throat or maybe a bad cold. Even in a place like Langley, they can't send a sick girl to school.

The principal sent a letter. WELCOME TO MEADOWLAWN SCHOOL. They make you take a school bus. No one will sit next to me or talk to me, which is all my mother's fault. SHE doesn't care that I am miserable in Texas. SHE doesn't care that I will never have a best friend – or any friend – for the rest of my life. All SHE cares about is her new husband PRINCE CHARMING. And now she is learning to milk cows. Isn't that crazy? She goes around in overalls that are baggy and bunchy like a man's overalls. She forgets about lipstick. She used to look pretty when we lived in the city. She always wore a dress.

MY MOTHER MAKES ME CRAZY MAD!

I am so scared about school. I hope my teacher is pretty. I hope she is nice. No one else will be (nice) to the new girl (me).

September 4, 6:00 A.M.

Mrs. Leitstein wrote me a letter! She wants to be my pen pal! I bet she misses me a lot. Well I miss her, and also her kitchen. Her house always smells good, like cookies in the oven. I wish I could go there tomorrow. We could drink cocoa and talk about things. Mrs. Leitstein is the best person to talk to when you have troubles. She knows exactly what to do. That's because she's old.

September 4, 1947

Dear Mrs. Leitstein,

I do not like Texas. They make you go to school when it still feels like summer. My room has tulip wallpaper. When you look out the window, there is nothing to see. Unless you like looking at a bunch of cows, *Mooooo!*

How are you? Now that we are pen pals, don't forget you have to write back right away please.

Thank you for the notebook that you gave me at the station. I love it! As you can see, I am using a piece of the paper to write you a letter. I write many things in my notebook. All of them are private.

Very truly yours,

Katie

Your pen pal Katie Roberts

I turn. I toss. I twist in my bed. Left side. Right side. Knees up. Knees down. Blanket up. Blanket down. Pillow puffy. Pillow flat. I lie on my stomach. I lie on my back. I CANNOT FALL ASLEEP! Why? Because tomorrow is the worst day of my life. My stomach hurts and my fingers are ice, but the rest of me is burning hot. Mama says she was always a nervous wreck, too, the night before the first day of school. Sam says take it from him, school is the best place to make friends. Grown-ups LOVE telling stories about themselves when YOU'RE the one who is crying and miserable. They want you to think they understand about being a child, but they don't understand anything. Well I hope and pray some girl, any girl, talks to me tomorrow. She doesn't even have to be best friend material. And I hope I'm not the tallest. What if I can't find Room 102 and I'm late and the teacher yells and I die of embarrassment in front of the whole class? What if I can't find the bathroom and I really need to go? And lunch . . . I can see myself now, ALL ALONE, me and my egg salad sandwich . . . I hope Mama puts a nice note in my lunch bag— that will cheer me up . . .

Good LucK KATIE. I sure do LoVE You! Mama

. . . Be right back . . .

I just snuck out of bed. Tried on my first-day-of-school clothes again. Mama made me a skirt with pleats for THE BAD DAY. It is plaid and I love it. New blouse, too. White. My shoes are not new, but I like them anyway. Brown with bouncing tassels.

If only I weren't so skinny. I eat and eat but all I get is tall. My father was tall. Handsome, too.

Here's what I wish. I wish I'd wake up tomorrow in my very own bed in my very own room in New York where there are double-decker buses and Macy's and no smelly cows. My father would be inside asking Mama for two socks that match. He would be shaving and singing. He always sang off-key.

I hope my wish comes true but I know it won't, good night.

September 6, 4:00 P.M.

Guess what? Mr. Keyes my teacher is a MAN! He is married to Mrs. Keyes the music teacher. A boy called Matthew sits behind me in the classroom. He talks and talks. I do not like boys.

Mr. Keyes

And I do not like being the new girl. My skirt is too short and my feet are too big and I miss my old school where everybody knows me. In this school I have nothing to say and no one to say it to. It's like my lips are glued together. Annie and Linda from my class sat across from me at lunch. Everything they said sounded like a secret. They were dressed EXACTLY the same. Same dress. Same socks. Same hair ribbons. Best friends, of course.

My reading book has a bright green cover with big gold circles. In science we learned about plant life in the desert. After that, a girl called Donna showed me all around the school. I bet you anything Mr. Keyes made her. Probably he feels sorry for the new girl. At recess everyone played around with everyone else. Except me. I sat on the grass near a tree, pretending to write in my notebook. I take it everywhere with me.

The school bus was bumpy. I sat alone.

MEADOWLAWN SCHOOL

Here is a picture of Meadowlawn School.
My room is marked with an X. This school is
brand-new. It is too big. A person could get
lost. There's a field out back, and also a pool.
I've never seen a school with a pool!
There's a swim team, too. Matthew told me.

September 10, 5:55 P.M.

My mother and I used to be together all the time
and we used to talk things over. We had no
secrets. Now, every time I want to be with her,
SAM shows up. I am TIRED of his face and I am
TIRED of sharing my mother.

Forget Annie. Forget Linda. Donna, too.
They've got a million friends already, so they
don't need me. Anyway they've all known each
other since first grade and it's not fair. I remember first grade. You have no troubles at all when
you are six. I would like to be little again, and cute.

But there is one girl . . . maybe maybe maybe . . . a friend for Katie. . . . Well I have my eye on this girl Lucie in my class. She has long, long, long blond hair and big black glasses. She wears overalls to school, and also checkered blouses. Mrs. Reidy the art teacher made us partners at a table. Lucie is a very good artist like me. I hope and pray she'll be my friend.

SUBJECT: GYM CLASS

They make you wear droopy, drippy, bagging bloomers. UGLY!

SUBJECT: LOCKER ROOM

I HATE changing in front of all those girls. I don't want anyone to see any part of me, so I change in a corner facing the wall.

SUBJECT: GOING HOME

I want to go HOME. I want to go there now, today, right this very minute. I could take a train all by myself, I know how to do it. No more Texas! My mother would be sorry, ha!

SUBJECT: MY MOTHER

Sometimes I think my mother likes Sam Gold more than she loved my father. She's always laughing when he's in the room. I don't know what's so funny.

<u>September 27, 8:00 P.M.</u>

My favorite thing in school is when Mr. Keyes reads from his fat book of short stories. I like the ones by Mr. O. Henry. This writer likes to trick you at the end. There's always a surprise. When I grow up, I am going to write stories that trick you at the end. Or I might be a famous swimmer.

It's really disgusting the way Pamela Greer is so popular. She's a show-off and a snob but everybody LOVES her. And guess what she wore all over her lips today? Lipstick! It was a really pale shade of pink, but I know lipstick when I see it. I also know you're not allowed to wear it in school and I hope she gets caught, ha! Of course EVERYONE wants to sit next to Pamela at lunch, but LA QUEEN gets to choose. I wonder if she'll ever choose me?

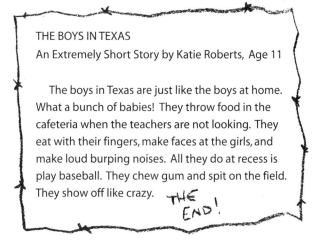

THE BOYS IN TEXAS
An Extremely Short Story by Katie Roberts, Age 11

The boys in Texas are just like the boys at home. What a bunch of babies! They throw food in the cafeteria when the teachers are not looking. They eat with their fingers, make faces at the girls, and make loud burping noises. All they do at recess is play baseball. They chew gum and spit on the field. They show off like crazy. THE END!

Introducing Miss Paulette . . . one day old! Our
new baby calf is the sweetest little baby in the
world! I was supposed to watch her get born but
I was in school when it happened. I am very mad
about that, but Miss Paulette is SO CUTE! Her
ears are flappy like puppy ears. Her eyes are big
and brown. Secret . . . I went to see her in the
barn in my pajamas when no one else was up.
Just me and Paulette all by ourselves at sunrise.
Paulette likes me. I told her I'll come back tomorrow. I told her we'll be secret pals.

Paulette

Paulette pays attention to everything
I say. She likes to hear about city things,
so I talk about the Empire State Building
and taxicabs and bagels. I tell how you
can ride the subway all day long for only
a nickel, on yellow seats that are made of
straw. I tell about surprise April blizzards,
and making snowmen in the park.

I can hear my mother and Sam in the kitchen.
Sam likes to make us pancakes in the morning.
He flips them high up. Sam thinks he's so great.
My mother never ate such great big giant break-
fasts in New York. She had normal things, such
as toast with tea. Now she drinks MILK, on
account of all those cows.

October 14, 1947

Dear Mrs. Leitstein,

Thank you for your letter. I love when there is something in the mailbox for ME!

Now I am going to tell you all the news from Texas. First, school: There are 14 girls and 16 boys in my class. Here are the girls: Lucie, Linda, Annie, Judy, Pamela, Wanda, Wendy, Gloria, Thelma, Maggie, Mindy, Deborah, Donna, and me, Katie. (I will tell you the boy names another time maybe). I am good in spelling, reading, and geography. Medium in science. Not good in arithmetic, which is a totally boring subject anyway. I like my teacher Mr. Keyes. I do NOT like the cafeteria. It is too noisy, and everyone sits with a best friend except me. I wish I could go home for lunch, but we live too far. In case you forgot, I had plenty of friends in my school in New York City. In New York I was practically popular.

I am thinking about sending you a present. When is your birthday, Mrs. Leitstein? How old are you?

Guess what — Mama milks cows! It is fun to watch but I will never do it myself. Yesterday Mama had tea with a bunch of Langley ladies. She changed her blouse 3 times before they came. The ladies liked her, so now she has friends and a new husband and I have no one. But don't worry, I am fine.

I made the school swim team! Our bathing suits are royal blue.

Don't forget to write to your pen pal soon soon soon!

Sincerely yours, *Katie*

Your faithful pen pal Katie Roberts

my friend
* LUCIE *

Well Notebook, here I am again — it's me
Katie Roberts, and something wonderful happened today. What happened is this: I MADE A
FRIEND! It's Lucie from my class, and she likes
me. She asked could she sit with me at lunch,
isn't that the best news in the world! All my
troubles are over. We talked so much, I nearly
forgot to eat. Not Lucie. Boy can she eat! Two
sandwiches, one peach, five chocolate cookies . . .
all that food and she is skinny like a rail. Skinny
like me. Lucie loves to tell jokes. She's got this
little book of them that she hides in her pocket.
Most people think she makes up the jokes, but
now I know the truth. I was scared she would
leave me for her other friends like Thelma and
Deb at recess, but we played catch. To tell you
the truth, Lucie did most of the catching and I
did most of the missing. Then I got a case of the
giggles and Lucie did, too. We just kept laughing,
it was so much fun. After that we watched the
boys on the baseball field. Lucie wanted to play
not watch, but they wouldn't let her. If I were
Lucie, I'd stay far away from boys.

   Now hear this . . . Sam is teaching Mama how
to drive! If you ask me, she will never get it right.
There's a dirt road in front of the house where

they practice. I like to sit on the fence and watch. This is better than the circus! I can hear my mother in a temper. Sam sounds stern. Sometimes he laughs. Whenever he starts laughing, I do, too. Not Mama. She just gets mad.

Here's a picture →

So I guess this has been a pretty good day in Texas.

November 4, 8:00 A.M.

It is Sunday and I am lounging in my pajamas in my room. I love to read under the covers, and I love to write in my notebook. When I grow up, servants will bring me breakfast on a tray every day. Of course I will live in the city, not Texas. I will be a famous writer of important books. My books will be in the library and I will also swim in the Olympics. Miss Paulette will have a room all to herself. She will be the most famous and the most beautiful cow in New York City. We'll take long walks in Riverside Park, and people will snap our picture. Paulette will nibble the grass and city children will pet her, and she will say *Mooooo!*

Mama, the boss of the world, just came by. "Get up, Katie love! Get dressed for Hebrew school!" Well, I don't WANT to get all dressed and I don't WANT to go to boring Hebrew school. Sam drives me over. We have to go a million miles to Temple Emmanuel so I can learn all about being Jewish, even though I already know all about it from my GOOD Hebrew school in New York. Anyway, I get to sit in front, and Sam talks the whole time. He likes to talk about my mother.

All dressed up for temple.

Sam ↑   Me ⌐   Mama ⌐

I am in a VERY BAD MOOD. Why? Because
Lucie who used to be my friend isn't (my friend)
anymore. We had a fight and now I have no one
and I hate this place.

NOSY. That's what she is . . . "Don't you LOVE
Langley, Katie? How come your parents don't
take you to church on Sunday? Don't you LOVE
living in Texas?" Jewish people go to <u>synagogue,</u>
not church, don't you know anything, I said.
Then I said New York is my REAL home and it's
great there. Texas is NOTHING like New York, I
said, and my mother MADE me move here — it
was entirely her idea not mine.

Then I told about Sam's ranch and the cows.
Then — it just slipped out — I said Sam isn't my
father. My father, I said, was a genuine hero who
died in the war. After that, stupid me started to
cry. I ran out of the cafeteria and hid in the girls'
room. So now Lucie thinks I'm just a big baby.
Not that I care. I don't like Lucie anymore. SHE
IS MUCH TOO NOSY. I guess I'll be looking for
a new friend tomorrow. Maybe Maggie.

I <u>HATE</u> THIS PLACE!

November 6, 12:30 P.M.

I am sitting on the grass near a tree in the schoolyard. Alone again. Just me and my notebook at recess. My friendship with Lucie is definitely over. She ate lunch with PAMELA of all people. Well fine! They can be best friends for all I care. Lucie didn't say one single word to me in art. I didn't say anything, either. The picture I made was really bad.

4:30 P.M.

Hello again, Notebook, it's me, Katie-who-has-no-friends. But! I have a job! Sam asked me to paint the fence in front of our house . . . and he is going to pay me some money. You know what I could do with my money? Buy two train tickets, ha! I'm tired of this place. It's not fair that I have to live here just because my mother thinks it's a good idea. We ought to go HOME, just the two of us. Sam can visit. Or, he can stay right here with his cows. If Mama won't come, I'll go alone. Although, a train ride to New York all by myself sounds a little scary.

Anyway, about the fence, Sam says I can choose any color I want, so I am choosing white. Although, I certainly like the color green. Maybe a green fence would be better. Bright kelly green, whoa! Monday after school we are driving to town to buy paint and paintbrushes. I can't wait to get started.

The one
and only
Katie Roberts
GIRL PAINTER

7:15 P.M.

. . . . Guess what! Lucie called! She told me a joke. Then she said, "I am sorry I made you cry yesterday." After that she sighed this great big sigh into the telephone and said she hopes her father never dies. I said I hope so, too.

November 7, 5:55 P.M.

School was a whole lot better today. Why? Because Lucie and I are friends again! We passed notes under the table in art and didn't get caught, whew! We swapped lunches. (I hope Pamela saw that, ha!) Lucie's mom makes great bologna sandwiches. Good news: I got 100% on a spelling test. (Lucie got 96). Not-so-good news: 72 in arithmetic. Mr. Keyes says come in for extra help, but I don't need extra help. I am very mad about that grade. It isn't fair he gave me such a bad grade. (Lucie got 90.) I wish I got 91, and that's all I have to say about boring old arithmetic.

Katie   Lucie

Here we are, two good friends, Katie and Lucie at recess. We are watching the boys play baseball. It is always our class against Mrs. Melby's, and ours is always the big loser. Day after day . . . Strike one! Strike two! Three strikes you're out . . . Lucie calls them PITIFUL. If they'd let HER play, she says, our class would win for a change.

Lucie likes Mindy and Thelma. They take the same school bus, and sometimes they go to each other's houses. I wish someone would invite me.

The swim team practiced after school. Maggie
from my class was there, too. You can tell she
feels funny in a bathing suit. You can tell from
the way she holds her arms. Folded — like a big X
across the front of her.

But boy is she fast! I was hoping I would be the
fastest swimmer on the team. If I were, then
everyone would like me. Miss Mack makes us
swim a million laps, and the water is VERY cold,
and you have to wear a tight white cap, and you
shiver like crazy when you get out. I love it!
Maggie says she's going to swim in the Olympics
when she grows up. Or she might work in the
rodeo.

I have to go . . . Mama's lighting the Sabbath
candles. Every Friday night she makes a special
dinner. We use the good dishes. She brought
them all the way to Texas, and the lacy tablecloth,
too. It used to be her mother's. I love Friday night
and the smell of chicken roasting in the oven.

Bye for now . . . .

Mr. Keyes chose ME ME ME to be editor of the class newspaper! In other words, I'm the boss, ha!

In honor of Thanksgiving, we made paper turkeys. Mine is purple, and he won't stand up. We're having a play for the parents. I told Mr. Keyes please don't make me be a Pilgrim all dressed up on stage. Put me on stage, I said, and I'll FAINT, or worse. Well Mr. Keyes is such a great teacher that he's letting me paint scenery instead. Lucie, too. But also two boys called Joseph and Bob.

I wish it would get cold. Thanksgiving is supposed to be grim and gray, and you're supposed to wear a coat. I miss the big parade in New York. My father always took me there on the subway. We'd go early in the morning, while they were still setting up, and stay until the very end. I remember hot chocolate and soft pretzels, Mickey Mouse and Santa Claus. I remember my father's muffler. It was blue.

November 24

Dear Mrs. Leitstein,

68 is not too old. Don't worry. My mother is 34. I am 11. I will try to remember to send you a present for your birthday on July 19.

I can picture you in your kitchen. You are making chicken soup. You are baking cookies, and outside there's a snowstorm. The window ledge is snowy white, but your dress is pink, and so is your sweater. You look very pretty.

I wish I could see you again. We had good times. I loved when you came for dinner, you always wore those pearls. Remember Mama's friend, Louise, the time her baby Rosie was born in a blizzard? I'll never forget that day! But now we're here in Texas, Mama is married to Louise's brother Sam, and you are far away. Are you ever lonely, Mrs. Leitstein? Maybe I can come over and cheer you up. I'll take the train. It is a very long ride, but I don't mind. Because there are berths just for sleeping, and a fancy dining car, too.

This house has a front porch with wicker chairs. Sam and Mama sit there drinking lemonade after supper. They talk too much. My mother acts like she's always lived on a ranch instead of in the city. She acts like this is home.

Yours truly,

Katie

Your good friend and pen pal Katie Roberts

PS: Two things about school —
1. I am editor of our class newspaper!
        VERY IMPORTANT JOB
2. My favorite friend is Lucie. She is the best girl
baseball player I've ever seen. Although, I haven't
seen too many!

December 15, 7:00 P.M.

Tonight is the eighth and last night of Hanukkah.
All the candles are lit and glowy. My father used
to eat piles of potato pancakes on this holiday. If
I close my eyes, I can see him at our little kitchen
table, patting his stomach and saying I CAN'T
BELIEVE I ATE SO MANY PANCAKES! When I
grow up and write books, they will all have
happy endings. In my books the father comes
home from the war. He just walks in the door
one fine day in his handsome army clothes. He
sneaks up behind the little girl's mother who is
baking cupcakes and taps her on the shoulder.
They kiss a big movie kiss. After that the little
girl flies into his arms. And they all live happily

together for a long, long time. Possibly forever.

In Hebrew school we had a Hanukkah party. There are just six of us in the class, but it was fun. We sang, and there were grab-bag presents. I picked a pair of pencils. Sam drove me home as usual. We talked about being Jewish. Sam did most of the talking. Sam says you can live anywhere and still be who you are. You can even live in Texas.

I wish it would snow. Even one little flake would be nice. I suppose it never snows in Langley — isn't that sad?

December 19, 8:04 P.M.

OH NO, OH NO, OH NO —
MAMA'S GOING TO HAVE A BABY!

Well THEY think this is the greatest news in the world, but I think it's the WORST. Mama's too old and anyway she's got ME to take care of. What about ME? And Sam Gold doesn't know the first thing about babies or children. All he knows about is COWS. My father knew EVERY-

THING about babies and children. Grown-ups are ridiculous. They think they're so smart, but they do everything wrong.

☆ This is how Mama will look. Her stomach will be FAT, which it already is on account of all those pancakes. Well if she wants to go around looking like THAT, fine. I don't care. Not one little bit.

☆ *Mama pregnant!*

10:15 P.M,

Hello again, Notebook. I cannot fall asleep because I am thinking. I am thinking and thinking. Why can't certain people leave things alone? Just when I am beginning to get a tiny bit used to living here, they go and spoil it. They never care about MY feelings. They only care about themselves. A baby. Who in the world needs that? And by the way, why would anyone pay attention to ME when there's a brand-new baby in the house? Babies are cute, and I am not. It's not fair. And I WON'T babysit, no matter how much they beg. I won't share my room, either, so they better not ask. This house is big, but it's not big enough for Baby and me. I wonder if it's going to be a boy baby or a girl? It better be a girl.

December 22, 6:00A.M.

I told Paulette she's not going to be the only baby in town but she'll always be MY baby and I will NEVER stop paying attention to her. When I got back from the barn, Mama was in the kitchen in her old striped pajamas. She used to wear them in the city. Sometimes we had breakfast parties on her big bed in the morning in pajamas. Just the two of us — no Sam, no baby. I was remembering those good times, so I wanted to say something kind and sweet, such as GOOD MORNING MAMA, MAY I HELP YOU WASH THE DISHES BECAUSE I LOVE YOU SO MUCH? but another part of me wanted to say something mean, such as HOW COULD YOU DO THIS TO ME? YOU'RE THE WORST MOTHER IN THE WORLD! I wanted to give her a big hug and ask her to read me a story the way she used to, but another part of me wanted to yell WHAT WOULD DADDY SAY? I couldn't decide what to do, so I came straight to my room to write in my notebook. I am so confused.

Today is the last day of school before Christmas vacation. All the girls are getting dressed up for a special assembly. The boys are wearing ties! I feel funny going to a Christmas assembly. Lucie says don't worry, Wendy's Jewish, too, and David. Sam and Mama are always telling me, be proud of your Jewish roots, and I am, but I do not like being different. I want to be like everyone else. So I will sing Christmas carols and eat Santa Claus cookies.

I am making a list of things I like about Texas.

1. LUCIE

2. MISS PAULETTE

3. MR. KEYES (except arithmetic)

4. MISS MACK my swim coach. Miss Mack likes to call me her City Swimmer. She likes to talk about New York because she is planning to go there one day. To be a Broadway star.

5. THE LANGLEY PUBLIC LIBRARY, which looks like someone's old house. My library card is yellow.

Flash! LUCIE INVITED ME TO HER HOUSE! I am so excited! Sam and Mama will drive me over at noon. I don't know what to wear. I don't know how to comb my hair. What if her mother makes something horrible for lunch that I hate? What if Mindy is there, or Thelma? I bet Lucie's parents made her invite me because they feel sorry for the new girl, sorry for a girl who doesn't know the words to ordinary Christmas songs. Maybe I'll stay home and help around the ranch today. I can learn to milk cows. Sam would like that. I can write all day in my notebook. Or type a story on Sam's typewriter which I am allowed to use anytime I want. My story will have a surprise ending. It will be about a girl swimmer who does champion swan dives, and every single person in school wants to be her best friend.

7:30 P.M. ❋ FUN!

Well I went to Lucie's, and guess what — it was SO MUCH FUN! She has four brothers and also a big sister Jennie, who is ABSOLUTELY GORGEOUS. I wish I looked just like her. Lucie says boys are always falling in love with Jennie.

Lucie's mom has curly blond hair. She is very sweet, and she never lectures Lucie the way my mother lectures me all day long . . . DON'T-POUT-KATIE and IT'S-TIME-YOU-START-THINKING-ABOUT-SOMEONE-BESIDES-YOUR-SELF-KATIE and HOW-ABOUT-A-LITTLE-HELP-AROUND-HERE-SUCH-AS-FOLD-ING-THE-LAUNDRY-KATIE. Lucie's father looks like a genuine cowboy with leather boots, but he may be a doctor, I think. They have a wonderful Christmas tree there. Lucie has a new doll called Beatrice with a beautiful porcelain face. We made a bed from a shoebox and changed Bea's clothes and pushed her all around in a real baby carriage. I felt funny playing with a doll. After all I'm eleven not seven. But who cares about that, because we had a really good time.

And one more thing. Lucie who loves baseball wants me to love it, too. So we got to work. Throw the ball. Catch it . . . catch it . . . oh, no . . . miss! Throw the ball. Catch it . . . catch it . . . oh, no . . . miss! Lucie's brothers tried to help. Jennie, too. I was PITIFUL. Then the littlest brother brought out a bat. He showed me how to swing. And you won't believe this — Katie Roberts WHACKED the ball over a fence! Beginner's luck, I guess.

January 2, 8:15 P.M.

Back to school and back to arithmetic and back to MEAN Mr. Keyes who made me miss recess today just because HE thought I needed to work on word problems. I DO NOT LIKE ARITH-METIC AND ESPECIALLY WORD PROBLEMS!

Terrible news . . . I think I am beginning to develop in certain places. I never thought it would happen to me, and I am mad. I'm only a little girl, you know. Only 11. And now I am looking bumpy and strange. Especially in my bathing suit. I might just quit the swim team if this keeps up, although my team really needs me.

January 20, 7:30 P.M.

Our class newspaper is called *Talk of the Town* and the first edition is EXCELLENT. Thanks to the excellent editor, me!

The editor gets to choose articles. There's only room for 8.

My article is on page 1. It is called "City Girl."

Matthew says it isn't fair that I'm the editor AND my article is on page 1. He's mad because I didn't pick his, but why should I? Nobody wants to read his totally BORING baseball story. I told him to write about something else next time, and don't make it boring. Matthew is so rude. He said since I like the city so much, how come I don't go back? So I said I wish I could, because this place is the WORST place in the world.

Boys are such a pain. Especially Matthew.

January 27, 10:05 P.M.

I am all by myself in the house because Sam drove Mama to school for Open House. I am waiting up because I have to hear every single thing Mr. Keyes said about me. I am in my bed with the covers pulled high. I wish they'd get home. I turned on all the lights in the living room and kitchen. I turned on every lamp in Mama's room, the guest room, and mine. If it weren't so dark outside, I would go to the barn to visit Paulette. But I am scared. This house is

too big, and there are strange night noises, and I
wish my mother would come home NOW.

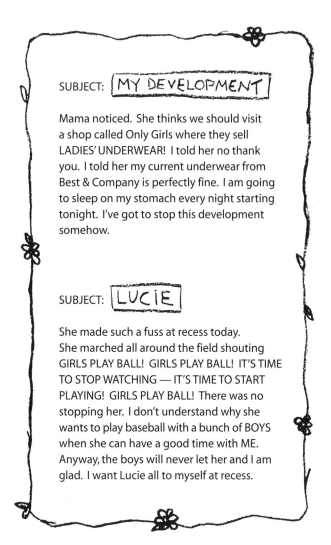

SUBJECT: MY DEVELOPMENT

Mama noticed. She thinks we should visit
a shop called Only Girls where they sell
LADIES' UNDERWEAR! I told her no thank
you. I told her my current underwear from
Best & Company is perfectly fine. I am going
to sleep on my stomach every night starting
tonight. I've got to stop this development
somehow.

SUBJECT: LUCIE

She made such a fuss at recess today.
She marched all around the field shouting
GIRLS PLAY BALL! GIRLS PLAY BALL! IT'S TIME
TO STOP WATCHING — IT'S TIME TO START
PLAYING! GIRLS PLAY BALL! There was no
stopping her. I don't understand why she
wants to play baseball with a bunch of BOYS
when she can have a good time with ME.
Anyway, the boys will never let her and I am
glad. I want Lucie all to myself at recess.

10:30 P.M.

I am soooooo tired. They're home and it's about time. Mama came straight to my room. She fluffed my pillow and brushed my hair and said a bunch of things that mean I AM VERY PROUD OF YOU KATIE. I guess Mr. Keyes told her all the right things about all my best subjects. I guess he forgot to talk about math. Good old Mr. Keyes. Good night!

February 10, 5:30 P.M.

I wrote an article called "My Friend Mrs. Leitstein" for *Talk of the Town*. It is a good article. I put it on page 1.

Matthew wrote about BASEBALL again. He is so stubborn. There's this player he loves called Joe DiMaggio. I bet no one cares about Joe DiMaggio except Matthew, but I chose it for page 8, which is the last page. Now Matthew can quit complaining.

February 18, 1948

Dear Mrs. Leitstein,

   Thank you for the picture that you sent me of
you. I will keep it always!

   I am so mad at my teacher Mr. Keyes. He is
making a boy in my class called Matthew help
me with word problems. So it's me and Matthew
the arithmetic wizard every Tuesday, starting
tomorrow. Mr. Keyes is the meanest teacher in
Texas, and the world.

   My mother failed her driver's test. She is very
mad! But you know my mother, she never gives
up. She is going to practice and practice, then
take that test again.

   Yesterday my friend Lucie came over. We
baked brownies. I showed her the best baby calf,
Miss Paulette. We sat in the hay in the barn drawing pictures. I drew one of you.

Sincerely yours,

Katie

Your pen pal Katie Roberts

Mrs. Leitstein ↑

February 19, 9:07 P.M.

Well the arithmetic genius Matthew blabs on and on about his favorite baseball team, the Yankees. I don't know why he has to tell me every single thing about every Yankee in the world or the Bronx. Matthew mows lawns around Langley. He is saving up for a trip to Yankee Stadium. All that work just to watch a game, and get Joe DiMaggio's autograph! Anyway I told him I know how to get there on the subway. Of course Matthew doesn't know about underground trains. So I sketched a little picture.

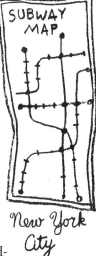

SECRET... Matthew is kind of sort of cute. Considering he's a boy. Black hair, freckles across his nose. Blue-green eyes. Well it's a good thing I lock up this notebook so no one can see what's inside. For example, right this second my face is BRIGHT BLUSH-ING RED! Isn't that dumb? I don't even LIKE Matthew. He is the most boring arithmetic tutor in the state of Texas. He makes me yawn.

February 24, 1948

Dear Mrs. Leitstein,

   I have a problem. Sam Gold wants to ADOPT me.
In other words I would be his child. My mother
ALWAYS sides with him, especially now that she is
going to have a baby, and she never sides with me.
She says Sam wants to take care of me as if I were
his own daughter. Well too bad! Because Sam Gold
is NOT my father, and that's all there is to it.
   Pen pals should sometimes tell a secret. I will
now tell mine. Sometimes I get so mad at my
father. It's all his fault I am stuck in Texas. It's his
fault about Mama's fat stomach. It's his fault Sam
wants to adopt me and change my name to yucky
Katie Gold. If my father didn't die in that war, then
Mama would still be married to him NOT Sam Gold,
and they wouldn't be fixing up a nursery with
teddy-bear wallpaper. I am very mad at my father,
but I wish I could hug him and kiss his cheek and
smell his after-shave. Isn't that crazy?

Signed,

Katie

Your No–Adopt Pen Pal
Katie Roberts

PS: If you have a secret, you should tell it to me.

February 26, 8:30 P.M.

Tuesday again. Math and Matthew, ha ha ha. We do a little arithmetic, but mostly Matthew talks. Mostly he talks about himself. Today he bragged about his secret trip to Yankee Stadium. He's been saving up for weeks. He keeps his money in a private box that he hides in the back of his closet. If I breathe a word to anyone, he says, I'm in big trouble. I love secrets! So this is the plan according to Matthew.

1. He is going ALL BY HIMSELF, ALONE!

2. But not until April when it is baseball season.

3. His parents love to worry, so there will be a farewell note on his pillow. He already wrote the note, and he keeps it in the closet in the same box with his money.

Well I guess you could say Matthew thinks of everything. If I had money, I'd take a secret trip, too. First stop, New York City! Then Alaska, which we are learning about in geography. In Alaska you go around on a sled. Husky dogs pull you fast through the snow, and you get to sleep in igloos.

I am sorry to say Lucie and I are in a fight, all because of this crazy story she wrote for _Talk of the Town_. "Girls Pitch, Too." Lucie thinks her story is so great. She says it HAS to go on page 1. I am sick and tired of talking about BASE-BALL, I said. Then Lucie said _she's_ sick and tired of hearing about NEW YORK — all I ever talk about is New York. Isn't that nasty?

And now thanks to Lucie there's a new base-ball team — all girls. And guess who made herself captain — LUCIE, of course. I WON'T be on her team. And I WON'T put her article on page 1, or any page. I'm the editor, don't forget. I am BOSS.

Everything is terrible.

I AM BOSS!
me! me!
me!

March 2, 1948

Dear Mrs. Leitstein,

   I am surprised you are siding with my mother. How
can you be so sure Sam loves me? Anyway I don't love
him. I like him, that's it. Here's what I like.
   1. Sam tells funny stories and his pancakes aren't bad.
   2. He lights a fire in the fireplace on chilly nights.
   (I snuggle with Mama on the couch. Whenever I put my
   hand on her stomach, the baby kicks, which feels very
   funny!)
   3. Sometimes he reads out loud from one of his millions
   of books. He wears silly red socks instead of slippers
   and you can see his toes wriggling inside.
   4. Sam can always get Mama to laugh. Even when she
   is complaining about being TOO big and TOO tired.
   So as you can see, Sam Gold is very nice. I like him and
he likes me, but he is not my family. He is not my father.
No adoption!
   Lucie who used to be my best friend is captain of her
girls-only baseball team. All of a sudden all the girls in all
the 6th grade classes are busy playing baseball. Except
me. I'll never waste my recess on a game like that.
   I bet you miss me. You must be very lonely. In case you
are wondering, I am old enough to travel on a train by
myself. Actually I am quite grown up. Who knows, I might
just hop on a train one of these days . . . I might just come
for a visit. No one here would miss me.

Signed your old neighbor and favorite pen pal,

Katie

Katie Roberts, age 11

March 5, 6:30 P.M.

My throat hurt in the morning.
Fever, too. No school! It was raining buckets all
day, and gray and cold. I slept, woke up, slept,
woke up. Mama came by with tea and home-
made sugar cookies. She smoothed my sheets
and brushed my hair and felt my forehead and
called Dr. Mason twice. In the afternoon we
looked at old pictures in an album. Just the two
of us, like old times. We cried a little and sometimes we laughed, when we looked at pictures of
my father. Mama misses him like I do. Cinna-
mon toast on a tray for supper. Sam brought a
rose from the garden. It opened right up while I
sipped my tea. You could hear the rain on the
roof. You could see it on the windows.

March 8, 5:00 P.M.

I went back to school today. It felt like the first day
all over again. No friends. No Lucie. I was behind
in reading and science, so I had to stay in at
recess. Which was just as well, since every single

44

6th grader in this school is baseball-crazy. I could see the fields from the classroom. Girls on one field. Boys on the other. Everyone screaming. Yelling. Cheering. I wanted to go home. I wanted to be with my mother. Mr. Keyes ate lunch at his desk. I pretended to do questions in my science workbook, but I kept on looking out the window. I kept my eye on Lucie. One time she struck out, and I was glad. Which made me feel awful, like the meanest girl on earth, which I probably am. I started to cry. Mr. Keyes was nice. He shared a cupcake from his lunchbox. Chocolate. I told him I have no friends. He said you have to BE a friend to HAVE a friend. Those words keep swirling in my head . . . you have to BE a friend to HAVE a friend . . .

cupcake

So now I have a surprise for Lucie. I am putting "Girls Pitch, Too" in the class newspaper. I am putting it right on page 1. Aren't I nice! Aren't I wonderful! To tell you the truth, it's a very good story. Everyone will read it.

I couldn't keep it secret another
SECOND so I wrote Lucie a note during art.
I told her the surprise about "Girls Pitch, Too."
She jumped off the art stool and gave me
a hug and said I'm the BEST friend a person
could ask for and I said I know! Mrs. Reidy
said RETURN TO YOUR SEAT IMMEDIATELY,
and the whole class laughed, but I didn't mind.
Neither did Lucie. We are friends again — we
are friends!

I am sitting way up high on the bleachers.
The rest of the world plays baseball. They shout.
They hoot. They howl and boo and grunt. Even
Pamela, La Queen. Lucie is boss of this field,
though. Right now she is trying to boss me into
playing but I have a case of the giggles, and
anyway I am writing in my notebook. I
promised Lucie I will play. But just a
little, and not every single day.

March 14, 5:30 P.M. ∨∕ ∕∕∕ ∕∕╱ ∕∕∕ ∕∕╱╱

Hello Notebook, guess what! Matthew needs an assistant. Which is why I get to mow lawns around Langley! Of course he gets to do the actual mowing, which everybody knows is the easy, fun part of the job. I do the raking. Not easy, but kind of fun for a city girl like me. Texas grass smells nice and sweet. You can sprinkle it in your hair, just for the heck of it. Matthew says I'm ridiculous. Too bad! By the way, I get 25 cents a lawn. I told Matthew it isn't fair that he gets 50 cents. He said take it or leave it. What a big shot.

March 16, 4:30 P.M.

Mama's stomach is popping out of all her clothes and she can't bend down! Lucie says you're never lonely when there's another child in the house and she is positive this baby is going to be a GIRL. One girl baby with green eyes and streaky blond hair, coming right up! In other words, she'll look like ME, ha! I like the name Lydia. But her other name will be Gold. Looks like I'll be the only one in this family with the last name Roberts. It's not fair. Unless Sam adopts me. Then . . . Katie Gold ???? . . . Katie Roberts . . .

And one more thing. If Sam adopts me, what do I call him?

Daddy.   No!

Dad.   No!

Father.   No!

Mr. Gold.   Maybe.

Sam.

His name is Sam and that's all there is to it. I am so confused. I have too many problems, it isn't fair.

March 21, 5:00 P.M.

This is a picture of me on my beautiful, new, gorgeous, green bicycle. A present from Mama and Sam, and it isn't even my birthday! I am riding to Matthew's house. His mother makes lemonade. Then we go around his neighborhood mowing and raking the lawns. What a team!

Here's Sam, showing me how to milk a cow. *Squirt, squirt!*
City Girl Milks Cows! Sometimes I miss New York, I tell Sam.
He looks sad, so I say, other times I nearly like it here. Now
Sam smiles. Then I ask, how come you married my mother?
Sam says these exact words: I love her, Katie, and I love you,
too.

That's me . . .
running out of the barn.
I run very fast.

March 28, 10:30 P.M.

I'M IN TROUBLE WITH THE LAW!
(my mother)

Here's what happened. Lucie came over after
school. We made covers for our book reports,

which was fun. Then she brushed my hair into a French twist so I'd look grown up, like her sister Jennie. I tried doing hers. Too much hair. Then Lucie got this great idea. LET'S CUT MY HAIR! I WANT IT SHORT, CUT AWAY! So I did. We had so much fun, laughing like laughing hyenas – and all that long blond hair on my bedroom floor. Katie Roberts, Expert Barber! Does Lucie like her haircut? You better believe it. She loves that you can see her ears. And doesn't mind a bit about the crooked piece in back.

Now the bad part of this story. Lucie's mom had a fit. She even called Mama. So now I am punished, all because of a silly haircut that makes Lucie look a thousand times cuter anyway. I am banished to my room every day after school for a week, and also next weekend. No bicycle. No raking. No drives to town. No trips to Lucie's house, and she can't come here. It isn't fair.

April 4, 1948

Dear Mrs. Leitstein,

I am punished. All I did was give my friend Lucie a sweet little haircut. I know it's not the best haircut in the world, but Lucie likes it fine. Grown-ups get grumpy about the silliest things. They act like they are perfect, but they're not.

By the way, I'm a working girl now. My job is mowing lawns. Actually a boy called Matthew gets to mow. I rake it all up and put the grass in baskets. I make a quarter a lawn. I guess you could say Matthew is my friend. Even though he's a boy.

I miss you so much, Mrs. Leitstein. You are the only grown-up who understands me. But don't worry about me, I am fine.

Yours truly,

Katie

Your pen pal in jail in her room, Katie Roberts

April 12, 7:30 P.M.

This is what I look like at the swim meet. I am the skinny one in Lane #3.

Swim, Katie, Swim!
Pull! Pull!
Touch the wall and flip . . .
Pull! Pull!
Elbows up!
Reach! Reach!
Go, Katie, go!

Well, Meadowlawn is the big winner this time. Sorry, Barnum Woods School. But we've got Katie Roberts on our team, La Champion!

After the meet, Sam and Mama take me to Flora's Ice Cream Shoppe on Main Street. We all have ice cream sodas.

April 14, 4:00 P.M.

TOP SECRET INFORMATION . . . . Matthew's
Aunt Gloria must be a millionaire. Because she
sent him ten dollars for his birthday. Sooooo
now he has enough money for his ticket to
Yankee Stadium! He even has extra. Matthew
really is excited. Imagine going on a train all
alone, and all the way to New York. I made
him a map. Aren't I terrific! This is where
you get off the train at Pennsylvania
Station. This is where you get the subway that will take you to Joe DiMaggio.
And this is where my friend Mrs. Leitstein
lives. Just knock on her door — she will cook
up a storm for supper. She makes wonderful
chicken soup, and she will tell you many stories.
Good ones, not the boring kind that parents tell.
And she will NEVER lecture. Matthew likes my
map. He folded it up and put it in his pocket for
safekeeping. I bet you anything he's scared.

But he wouldn't be (scared) if I went along.
Think of it! I could surprise Mrs. Leitstein. I'd
visit the library and the temple, and also my
school where all the girls would hug me. I could
swing on the swings in Riverside Park and watch
the Hudson River.

53

April 15, 1948

Dear Mrs. Leitstein,

Remember the boy Matthew I told you about?
Well guess what — he is coming to New York to
meet a famous man, Mr. Joe DiMaggio. The train
he is taking leaves Langley next Friday. Don't be
too surprised if Matthew rings your bell, because
I told him all about you. His hair is black and his
eyes are bluish-greenish, and he isn't bad to look
at. But beware, he will talk all day long about the
Yankees and baseball!

    By the way, two other girls in my class —
Pamela and Maggie — asked if I could cut their
hair like Lucie. I told them I'm not in the barber
business anymore, ha!

Your friend,

Katie

Katie Roberts

PS: Passover is coming. I wish I could come to
your house for the seder. Wouldn't that be fun!
We could light candles and eat matzo ball soup.
You wouldn't be lonely.

April 17, 9:30 P.M.

Hello Notebook, this is Katie Roberts, the most unloved girl in Texas and the world. Why? Because my own mother doesn't love me. She only loves SAM. And also that HATEFUL baby in her HUGE and HATEFUL stomach. Now I know the truth.

Here's what happened . . . Sam has been building this baby crib, a surprise for Mama. Every night after supper, he sneaks out to the toolshed to work on it. Tonight he finished. The crib is painted yellow. There are painted ducks, too, and wheels on the bottom so you can push it around. (I will never say it to Sam or my mother, but the crib he made is the most darling thing in the world.) Mama was out front hang-ing laundry on the line, so Sam and I carried it up the back steps. We rolled it right into the nursery, which is right next door to MY room of all places.

When Mama saw the crib, she started to cry. She cried and cried! Sam looked sad, like maybe he painted the ducks the wrong color. Finally my mother said . . . and I quote . . . I've never been so HAPPY in my whole life. . . . She said it only to SAM, and she patted her stomach, and she never once looked at ME. It was like I wasn't even in the room or the house or anywhere.

So now I know the truth about my mother. She loves Sam more than me. And she already loves that baby more than me, too.

I wish I could run away from this place and never come back. They can take their crib and their baby and have a great time without me. I wish I were six. Everything was wonderful when I was six.

I am going to bed and I WON'T say good night to them. I'll pretend I am sleeping when Mama comes in to kiss me. She always does that, and whispers, Sweet dreams, Katie. I don't know why she bothers — she doesn't even mean it. I'm just an obligation. Well fine! She can save up all her kisses for BABY. See if I care!

April 18, 5:45 A.M.

I've made my decision once and for all. I am going with Matthew. To New York. I can't wait to tell him. My mother will be sorry.

5:00 P.M.

Flash! Flash! Matthew says it's OK — I can go! He says I'm always talking about going there anyway, so this is my big chance. But I have to follow his rules and I have to keep it secret. Not a word to my mother. Or Lucie. My ticket costs a lot, so Matthew is giving me some of his birthday money. Well, isn't he nice!

I am so excited! Good-bye Texas, ha! I am going home! That Matthew is some good pal. This is the greatest day of my life. I have many things to do:

1. WRITE TO MRS. LEITSTEIN
   (or should I be a surprise?)

2. PACK RED VALISE, HIDE VALISE IN CLOSET
   pajamas
   plaid skirt
   toothbrush
   hairbrush
   bathing suit
   sandwich/cookies
   warm sweater, underwear, socks
   notebook!!!

3. WRITE A FAREWELL NOTE TO MAMA (and Sam?)

4. TELL LUCIE THE PLAN
   (I promised Matthew to keep it totally secret, but I've got to tell someone . . . and after all, Lucie is my best friend . . . but she better not tell a soul and especially not her mother.)

<u>*April 19, 4:30 P.M.*</u>

I told Lucie. I AM GOING TO NEW YORK WITH
MATTHEW, I said, AND THIS IS ABSOLUTELY
SECRET. She started to cry. Lucie thinks I'm
never coming back. She sniffled all through geography, then spelling. Mr. Keyes sent her to the
nurse, but of course she didn't have a fever. We
sat on the bleachers at recess. Lucie says if I
promise to come back to Langley, she promises
not to make me play baseball. I told her baseball
isn't too bad, if you're in the mood. I found this
note in my desk.

Roses are red
violets are blue
when you go away
I'll be thinking of
you
        Love,
            Lucie

I wrote one back.

Roses are handsome
Violets are pretty
You're my best friend
In Texas and New York City
            Love,
            Katie

April 19, 1948

Dear Mrs. Leitstein,

   Get ready for a wonderful surprise!

Signed,

Katie

Your pen pal Katie Roberts, world traveler

April 22, 11:30 P.M.

I am SO NERVOUS! Tomorrow is THE BIG DAY.
Mama will be sorry, but it's too late now. I
washed all the dishes tonight. Dried them, too,
and put them away. I folded my blouses and
made perfect piles in the drawer. I ironed every
single thing in the ironing basket. Mama sure
will miss all the millions of chores I do around
this house. She will miss me when I'm gone.

   Today she was getting ready for Passover. Our
first Texas Passover. I can't imagine this holiday

without her. Well too bad. Because I am going home. Next Friday night I can visit our old temple. Everyone there will be happy I'm back. They will say I look more like my father every day. I will tell them about Texas.

Dear Mama (and Sam),

I am going away, but don't worry. I have a chicken
sandwich and my toothbrush. I remembered a
warm sweater. Happy Passover.

   I wasn't planning to tell you where I am going,
but I changed my mind. I am going home. To New
York. I know you think Texas is perfect. It's not
terrible here. I like the ranch, Miss Paulette, and
school most days. I am glad Mama finally passed
her driving test. I will think of you often. The train
leaves Langley at 6:00 A.M. I will ride my
bicycle to the station. In New York I
will live with Mrs. Leitstein. She is
lonely and old. I can help her with things.
She misses me.

   Well I hope you and the baby are all
very happy together, which I know you
will be now that I'm not in the way. I will
write when I get settled. By the way,
Matthew from my class is coming along.
He has an appointment with Mr. Joe
DiMaggio.

Sincerely yours,

Katie

Katie Roberts

New York City

Langley

April 23, 6:00 A.M

Guess what, I am on the train to New York! My
fingers are shaking, and my hands. I might get
sick to my stomach but who cares, because here
I am sitting next to Matthew and we are going to
New York, ha! The whole time I was riding my
bicycle to the station on the dark road, I was
CRAZY-SCARED. But Matthew met me like we
planned and we hid our bikes in the bushes. The
train is long and silver. When the whistle blew,
all of me shivered. We told the conductor we
were going to our uncle's funeral. We pretended
to cry.

6:30 A.M.

First stop after Langley will be Little Creek Falls.
I am so excited. And SO SCARED — I don't know
why. I wonder if Mama read the note? I wonder if
she cried? I miss her. Isn't that crazy? I've never
been away from my mother before. Not over-
night. Well too bad! She should have paid more
attention to me.

6:40 A.M.

Matthew does not understand that I need quiet
when I am writing in my notebook. He keeps
talking. And punching his fist into the baseball
mitt DiMaggio's going to sign. How can I think
with all this noise? What I am thinking about is
living with Mrs. Leitstein for my whole entire
life. I couldn't do that. A year sounds good, or
maybe one week. It wouldn't be fair to Mama.
Sam might miss me, too. He's the one who wants
to adopt me, right? And take care of me like an
official daughter, right?

7:20 A.M.

Well, Matthew forgot his sandwich. I had to
share mine, and he was mad because he likes
scrambled eggs for breakfast, not chicken. Too
bad. I have some money in my pocket. I hope
there's enough for a glass of milk in the dining
car, and also the subway ride to Mrs. Leitstein's.
I hope she is home when we get to the City. I
wonder if Mama is worried. You're not supposed
to worry when you are going to have a baby. I
am trying not to cry. Matthew mustn't see me
cry. He will think I'm a coward. Which I am.
More later . . .

April 23, 8:20 P.M.

Hello Notebook, it's me Katie Roberts, age 11,
and I have so much to tell you! You can't believe
all the things that happened today. WE GOT
CAUGHT. Guess who was waiting at the station
when the train pulled into Little Creek Falls?
Sam. I was mad and glad at the same time, but I
only acted mad. Sam grabbed my valise and
Matthew's suitcase and we followed him off the
train. I felt like a criminal! Sam never said a word,
except HURRY. Then he pointed to his old black
car, which was parked at the station. Mama was
in the front seat. I wanted to jump in her lap and
hug her and tell her I was sorry. But I didn't do
any of those things. Because THEY had spoiled
my running away to New York. Then guess where
we went? STRAIGHT TO THE HOSPITAL
BECAUSE MAMA WAS GETTING READY TO
HAVE THE BABY THREE WEEKS EARLY!

The minute we got there, they took her away.
I didn't like that. Sam and Matthew and I went to
a waiting room to WAIT. I wanted to say something nice to Sam but I couldn't think what.
Matthew's parents came. His mother hugged him
so hard, I thought he might break. Then she
bawled him out like crazy and they went home. I
wanted MY mother. What was taking so long? It

shouldn't take so long just to have a baby. What if something was wrong? Mama could die. I started to cry. Sam held my hand. I didn't let go.

A long time later a nurse came by. Sam stood up. The nurse whispered in his ear. Sam sat down. Then he laughed. He laughed and laughed. TWINS! TWIN BOYS!

I HAVE TWIN BABY BROTHERS! They are the best little babies in the nursery or anywhere else in the universe for that matter. Their names are Billy and Seymour, and they are coming home with Mama in five days.

♡ ♥ I CAN'T WAIT! ♡

And one more thing. Mama and I made up. I love her so much and she loves me so much. I cried buckets when I finally got to see her. I just couldn't stop. Then we talked about everything. I told her she never pays attention to ME anymore and she only pays attention to SAM and they make me feel left out and I'm too tall and not cute at all. Then it was Mama's turn. She said I mope and pout and spend too much time feeling sorry for myself. She said I could try a little harder with Sam, for example. Then . . . Lecture #2000 . . . grown-ups have feelings, too, and you can't go through life pushing people away, people who love you. Then she promised to pay a lot of attention to me if I pay a lot of attention to Billy and Seymour.

April 24, 5:21 A.M.

I've been thinking about all the people in this house with one name and me with another. And I've been thinking about my father. What would he say? Adopt or no adopt? I bet he would like Sam. After all, Sam is watching out for us, right? Maybe my father would be happy Sam wants to take good care of me, since he can't be here to do it himself . . .

Katie's NO ADOPT *List*

1. Sam is NOT my father.
2. I need MY name because it is my father's name.
3. Katie Gold is a name that has nothing to do with me. Katie Roberts, Katie Roberts, THAT'S me!

Katie's **ADOPT** *List*

1. I like Sam.
2. Sam loves me!
3. I kind of sort of love Sam, maybe, <u>just a little.</u>

+ 4. Billy and Seymour
   5. Mama

=   One family

April 24, 8:10 P.M.

Sam and I ate sandwiches on the front porch for supper. There was a nice breeze. I told Sam he could adopt me if he still wants to, which he does. I told him I want to keep my own name, though, just the way it is. KATIE ROBERTS IS A BEAUTIFUL NAME. That's what Sam said. He kissed the top of my head.

Four long days until my mother and the babies are back on the ranch. How in the world can I possibly wait?

April 28, 1948

Dear Mrs. Leitstein,

Sam told me you called long-distance because you had a sneaky suspicion I was on my way to New York. I am sorry my visit did not work out, but it's a good thing I am here in Texas right now because . . . are you ready for this . . . we have twins! I was hoping for a girl, but Seymour and Billy are so incredibly wonderful. I love them to pieces even if they are boys. They came home from the hospital today. This house is crazy-wild!

Anyway, I am very good with babies, and they need me around here, so I won't be able to come to New York too soon. (Matthew isn't coming either, due to the fact that his parents won't let him go anywhere but school for the next six weeks.)

I am thinking two things.
   1. I wish my father could see the babies. I know he can't, but I bet he would sing them a silly song.
   2. I was wondering, how would you like to visit us HERE in Texas?!! I know this place takes getting used to, but really, it's not so bad. You could stay a week or a year — as long as you like. You can meet Lucie and Miss Paulette. I will show you my school and the library and a funny street called Main Street, which is nothing like Broadway. Please say yes! Just take the train from Pennsylvania Station and we will meet you at the

station in Langley. We'll all be there . . . Sam and
Mama, Seymour and Billy. And I will be there,
too, with the biggest hug you can imagine.
Please say yes!

Love and kisses,

Katie Roberts

Me, Katie Roberts, age 11

Love and Kisses XOXO

The Great Green
Notebook of
Katie Roberts
who just turned 12
on Monday

Dear Kate,

I love our long walks
and cozy talks. All the
rest of it, too.
Love, me,
Mommy
♡

And special warm thanks to Susan Halperin
—ALH

August 7, 1948

Dear Mrs. Leitstein,

Thank you for the GREAT green notebook that you sent me for my birthday—I LOVE IT, LOVE IT, LOVE IT! I can't wait to start writing lots of things inside, and filling it up with pictures.

Do you remember that red notebook, the one you gave me last year? That was the day Mama and I were moving to Texas. I was so scared. Remember how you came to the station to see us off? I felt sad waving to you, and you waved back, and your gloves looked like little white dots when the train pulled away. Anyway, about that notebook—the red one—how did you know I used up all the pages! For weeks and months I was writing millions of private things in there, and then one day—boohooo—no more pages. Guess what I am calling my new notebook? I am calling it THE GREAT GREEN NOTEBOOK OF KATIE ROBERTS, who just turned 12 on Monday. Well, I hope 12 is good and great, Mrs. Leitstein. So far it's kind of regular. A long time ago when you were 12, did anything interesting happen to you? Did you maybe like a boy, for example?

Very truly yours,

Katie ♡

Your friend (and pen pal) Katie Roberts, age 12

PS: When are you *ever* going to visit us in Texas? You keep saying one of these days, but so far, no Mrs. Leitstein. It's a long way from your house in New York to my house in Texas, but don't worry, you can read a book on the train. Or look out the window. The porter is nice! He wears a cap and helps you with your luggage.

<u>*August 7,* 7:00 A.M.</u>

This is it! *The Most Private Tree House* of Katie Roberts. No grownups! No babies! Selected visitors by invitation only! Sam built it just for me, for my birthday, and Mama sewed big pillows with my name stitched across, to make it nice and cozy.

NO GROWNUPS!

Hey Notebook! Here I am, it's me, Katie Roberts, sitting way up high in my tree house. I love it up here, but I'm still so bad at climbing. I keep scraping different parts of me on the way up, and also going down. Left knee, blood! Right arm, blood! Tiny pinky, blood! It's worth it, though, just to be ALONE. To be in a place where MY MOTHER isn't saying, "Do this, Katie, do that, Katie."

ANNOYING BOSSY MOTHER EXAMPLE #1

No fair! My whole entire life *she* made my bed, every single morning. Now—all because there are BABIES in this house—*I* have to make it. Every day, too, no matter how many important things I have to do. There are too many bumps

3

when I'm done, and my pillow's too flat, and the sheets hang down. Which never used to happen when Mama made the bed.

ANNOYING BOSSY MOTHER EXAMPLE #2

Shocking! Mean! Child labor! Who sets the table *and* clears the table *and* dries all the dishes? I do. Me. La Servant. And who drops a glass into 2 million pieces 2 times in a row? I do. Me. Miss Clumsy. Bossy Mother Speech #1 . . . "Careful, Katie!" #2 . . . "Again, Katie?" Then she scoops up the babies and hands *me* the broom. Just like Cinderella.

La Servant

Things to do in My Tree House:

1. Write in my brand-new, gorgeous-new, gorgeous-green notebook! Which comes all the way from New York and is a present from Mrs. Leitstein, who used to be our neighbor there. Mrs. L is old, but I don't mind. Because she's extra nice. Sometimes I tell her my problems. We are pen pals! PS: Everything I write in here is personal and private and all about me.

2. Eat cookies before breakfast!

3. Make secret anniversary present! Today is Mama's anniversary—married one whole year to Sam Gold. I like Sam. Sam likes me and loves me so much that now I am adopted. The day the papers got signed, we all went to town for ice cream sodas. I love coffee sodas best. A long time ago before he died in the war, my father loved them, too. We used to get them in a place called Schrafft's. That's in New York City.

   Uh-oh, here comes Mama . . . across the yard . . . down the sloping hill . . . one baby under each arm and calling, "Katie, come home for breakfast, Sam is making pancakes." Pancakes! I am sooo hungry and Sam's pancakes are sooo

good . . . Well, bye for now, Notebook
. . . and by the way, welcome to my life,
Notebook . . . I love you already!

August 7, 8:22 P.M.

Presenting Miss Katie Roberts,
the future Miss Texas, tra-laaa!

🌷 🌷 🌷 🌷

Hello, here I am again, Notebook, lounging
on my bed in my room with tulip wallpaper in
my favorite pajamas with pink hearts. My hair's
wrapped in a towel, and guess what I smell like?
Lemons and limes! Which is the smell of Mama's
new shampoo, which I just borrowed, ha! Instant
beauty . . . shiny hair, silky hair, a brand-new me.
Of course, SHE'S so busy with Sam she'll never
even notice. Can you believe they're *dancing,*
right there in public, on the front porch!
Anniversary dancing, yuck. At least anniversary
parties are fun. We had one in the kitchen
after supper.

The First-Anniversary Party of Mama and Sam

GUESTS: Me. Mama. Sam. Billy and Seymour.

Ooops!, I forgot to talk about my twin baby brothers . . . Presenting Billy! And Seymour! Cutest little babies in Texas! I'm an expert sister—ask anyone, even Mama. I hold them and feed them and help with the bath. But no diapers, not me. This is how I make them laugh: I sing and dance around. I make funny faces. Lucie, my best friend, has four brothers of her own, but she's in love with my twins. Whenever she comes over, she wants to play with them every single second. Which makes me mad sometimes.

CAKE:

Whipped cream, mmmnn, strawberries from Mama's garden, mmmnn.

PRESENTS:

1. Sweater for Sam. From Mama. She knit it herself for a big surprise, but hey, look what happened, the sleeves are too short! Sam? He doesn't care about too-short sleeves. He loves that sweater just the way it is. Mama made his favorite color, blue.

2. Book for Mama. From Sam. Too many poems inside, and Sam wrote a too-mushy message inside: "I'll always love you, my darling. Sam."

3. ✹ ✹ Special picture made by me! ✹ ✹
Mama and Sam love and adore my picture,
yo ho ho! It's a girl on a trolley car in the city. I
like to draw things I remember about New York.
Whenever I rode the trolley with my father, he
held my hand tight. So I wouldn't get lost.

August 14, 5:30 P.M.

Yeeoowww! Guess who was at the town pool
today? The one and only Matthew, who was in
my class last year and who better *not* be in my
class this year. He was eating a hot dog at the
snack bar, and I was pushing Billy and Seymour,
with everyone peeking in the carriage, saying,
"Aren't they adorable?" and I did NOT say hi (to
M). His bathing suit is horrid, with fat stripes.
I love my bathing suit. It is red. But I hate how I
look in it, so the second I'm out of the pool, I
put on my shirt and button every button. Why?
Because NO ONE, NO ONE, NO ONE is going
to see my development (in certain places), and
that's all there is to it.

Extremely private information: PRIVATE
I *used* to like M, sort of, when I was 11. I *used* to
think he was cute. We were friends. He helped

me with math sometimes, and I helped him mow lawns around Langley. Then he got this *bad* idea about running away to NY. All because he was dying to meet this famous baseball player, Joe DiMaggio who is a very famous Yankee. So, stupid me said I'd go, too, and there we were— ON THE TRAIN TO NEW YORK! Just the two of us, and I was scared and shaking. But then Sam and Mama showed up, and that was the end of running away. I can't believe I did such a dumb baby thing. Which is why I want to be invisible every time I see M—I want to disappear.

And one more thing. Matthew and I *used* to be the same height. Now look who's taller—I am. I wish I could shrink back to my old size. Mama's always saying, "Shoulders back, Katie. Stop slouching, Katie . . . " a million times a day. SHE thinks tall is good and great and you're supposed to be proud. Wrong, wrong, wrong!

The Mean Mother

a story by famous girl-author Katie Roberts

Once there was a girl and no one paid attention to her and it was a burning hot summer day and she was very bored (in Texas) and there was nothing to do (in Texas). So she said to her mother in a very sweet voice, "May we go to town?" Mother said, "Not now." The girl was sad. But she knew all about *cooperation* and that's why she dried hundreds of dishes and folded millions of diapers and swept the kitchen floor. After all that hard work, she said, "May we go now?" Mother said, "Billy has a runny nose! I have to make lunch! There's laundry to hang on the line!" The girl stamped her foot (a teeny little bit). Which Mother did not like. "You can't always get what you want the minute you want it," went the big speech. Well, little Cinderella girl ran to her room and slammed the door and flopped on her bed to be mad. And that is the story of The Mean Mother.

August 27, 4:23 P.M.

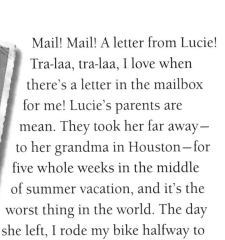

Lucie
Katie Roberts'
best friend

Mail! Mail! A letter from Lucie! Tra-laa, tra-laa, I love when there's a letter in the mailbox for me! Lucie's parents are mean. They took her far away— to her grandma in Houston—for five whole weeks in the middle of summer vacation, and it's the worst thing in the world. The day she left, I rode my bike halfway to her house, and she rode her bike halfway here. We sat under a tree and made a best-friends pact.

I, Katie, do hereby solemnly swear never to have another best friend, only Lucie.

I, Lucie, do hereby solemny swear never to have another best friend, only Katie.

So far, I wrote four letters to Lucie and she wrote four to me, and the best place to read them is my tree house, where it's **PRIVATE**. In Houston, Lucie gets to sleep in the bed her mother had when she was a little girl, and no one makes her

11

do chores. Okay, here's the best thing that happened to lucky Lucie (in Houston). THERE WAS A PARTY (with boys) AND A BOY ASKED LUCIE TO DANCE! I wish, wish, wish a boy would ask me to dance. And I wish Lucie would come home now, today, right this very minute. We have to decide what to wear the first day of school.

Blue skirt,
white blouse,
white socks?

Red skirt,
white blouse,
no socks?

Red skirt,
checkered blouse,
white socks?

ANNOYING BOSSY MOTHER EXAMPLE #3
Whenever you think your hair looks pretty, she says, "It's flopping in your eyes, Katie . . . way too straggly, Katie . . . you really need a trim." No, no, no!

August 28, 1948

Dear Mrs. Leitstein,

A long time ago when you were 12, did your
mother let you wear lipstick? Or, did she treat
you like a baby? MY mother treats me like a baby.
When school starts next week, all the girls will be
lipsticked but me. They'll be pretty and I'll look
like a little 1st grader.

I am sitting on the fence watching cows eat
grass and writing a letter to you. Sam is waving
from the tractor and Mama's pulling sheets off the
line. Two no-nap babies are playing on a blanket.
You should see our twins, Mrs. L! They are chubby
now, and a little fat, and sooo cute. They both have
curly brown hair, like Sam. They both have green
eyes. I have green eyes. Mama, too. Most people
don't know who's Billy and who's Seymour, but
here's a little secret. Billy has a freckle on his right
ear. And that's how you tell them apart!

Signed,

Katie

Katie Roberts, your mature
and growing-up pen pal

PS: Mama has three lipsticks in her top dresser
drawer, but she never remembers to wear them.
Except Friday night when she's all dressed up and
lighting Sabbath candles. My favorite color is
Ravishing Red — wow, is it red! Also, I like Paris Pink.

August 31, 6:00 A.M.

Big day! Great day! Going-to-town day!
Me and Mama only. No babies. No Sam. One
totally private day with my mother, coming
right up. Wake up, Mama. Wake up now so we
can go to town, and I'll wear my tall black boots
in the rain.

Here I am, all snuggled in my bed,
and I'm the first one up, and it is pouring
on the window. Just me and my old bear,
Cammy, and my secret shoe box, pssst,
look inside...Mama's old beads, 1 gold
key, 1 rose petal, and a picture, which I love.
Me when I was a baby! I love another one,
too. Me when I was 7, Mama, and my father
in his soldier clothes. Going-to-war clothes.
My dress in the picture is pretty, with pleats.
My father looks brave.

SPECIAL THINGS TO DO IN TOWN

1. School shoes. I want red velvets. With a little
   heel. There's a big snob, Pamela, who used to be
   in my class last year, and she has shoes like that.
   Of course, MAMA likes shoes that are sturdy, not
   pretty. Will Katie talk her mother into velvets?
   Yes. No. Maybe. Yes. No. Maybe.

2. Library. Return three books. Borrow three more. Miss Lewis knows my name, and sometimes I'm allowed to put picture books on the shelves. Important job.

3. Main Street Paper Shop. School supplies! New colored pencils! They have a typewriter in the window there, and I love it so much. Sam has a typewriter in a special black case. Sometimes when he isn't home, I go in his closet . . . shhh . . . open the case . . . shhh . . . sit on the floor, and pretend I'm that famous future writer Katie Roberts, writing my important book.
The thing I want most in the world is a boyfriend. After that, a typewriter of my own.

August 31, 4:00 P.M.

WATCH OUT: BAD MOOD.
Message from Katie in Bad Mood in Tree House.

Grownups. All they care about are cows. Babies. Mopping floors. They never care about me, I always come last. All I wanted was a special day with my mother, but everything went wrong. First a sick cow. Then Billy bumps his head and Mama blames *me*. ("I thought *you* were minding him, Katie.") Then a leaky roof, puddles on the kitchen floor, and *I* have to help with the mopping. I've been waiting and waiting all day long just to go to town, and all I do is wait. Mama says tomorrow's another day, but who cares about tomorrow? And one more thing, it's *meatloaf* for supper. Which I hate. I want new shoes, not meatloaf.

September 4, 7:00 P.M.

Yippiaaa, Lucie's home from Houston and it's about time! She came over, and the first thing after a million hugs was showing her my tree house. Which she loved and adored. Especially when she saw the sign I made. *Guest of Honor Lucie. Enter Best Friend Lucie.*

Lucie told me a secret. There's a boy with brown hair called Leo in Houston, and Lucie likes Leo! We made a list of all the things she likes about Mr. Wonderful.

1. Cute
2. CUTE
3. CUTE ♡

We were eating sandwiches with jam and looking at Mama's *McCall's* Magazine, then Lucie got
her big idea. Write a letter to Leo! We were writing and erasing and spilling purple jam all over
Leo's letter, and we couldn't stop laughing!
Finally, three perfect sentences in a row. Lucie
signed, "From your friend Lucie." Then she got
all worried, because what if Leo doesn't write
back? She was so sad about the letter that wasn't
coming that she started to cry, poor Lucie.

New shoes. In the shoe store Mama said "Absolutely
not!" when I showed her the most beautiful shoes in
the world. I was mad. I said, "If I can't have red velvets,
I don't want shoes!" Mama said, "Fine Katie, be my guest,
wear your old, too-tight shoes to 7th grade." Then I was
really mad. Then the man brought out navy blue loafers
with tiny slits for pennies, and it was love at first sight.
(Which I'm never saying to Mama.) Lucie loves my new
shoes, we were trying them on in the tree house. Lucie's
are brown. Not too pretty. Her mother made her get them.

September 5, 10:07 P.M.   SCHOOL ?

Mayday! Mayday! Tomorrow's the first day of
school! I'm so scared, my stomach is going crazy.
I practically couldn't eat dinner. My favorite
things, too. Spaghetti! Lemon meringue pie! And
how am I supposed to fall asleep when my eyes

keep popping open? I've tried everything so far. Warm bath. Read in bed. Shutters open. Shutters shut. Window up. Window down. Counting sheep. Counting worries.

Worry #1
What if my teachers don't like me?

Worry #2
What if everyone has a boyfriend but me?

Worry #3
What if Lucie finds a new best friend and I have no one? I have to find Mama. She'll know what to do. She always knows what to do.

September 5, 10:45 P.M.

Me and Mama drinking milk in the night in the kitchen with straws. We are having pie. Mama irons at night, and sometimes she bakes. The radio plays and she wears no shoes. We talk and talk, it reminds me of the old days. Before babies. Before Sam. I'm so full of pie, my stomach is sticking out. Good night, tummy-pie!

HEADLINE, HEADLINE: *Read All About It!*

Miss Katie Roberts, who used to be in 6th grade at Meadowlawn School, is now in 7th. Well done, Katie! More good news: Katie and best friend, Lucie, are in the same class! Room 202. They wear matching friendship rings and stay together every second, every minute, all day long.

We have Miss Casey for homeroom and language arts and math. I love Miss Casey! She's really pretty, and she smiled at me whenever I raised my hand. I raise my hand a lot in reading. I hope Miss Casey likes me. I want to be her favorite. Last year I had Mr. Keyes. Nice, but too strict about arithmetic. *Nice Girls in Room 202:* Me! Lucie! Maggie! Lara! Frances! *Snobby Girls in Room 202:* Pamela, Wendy, yuck! *Big Problem:* Why, why, why is Matthew in my class again, and why does he have to sit next to me? What a big talker and what a big pest! He has this picture of Joe DiMaggio. The picture's all dirty and crumpled, but Matthew thinks it's the greatest thing on earth. Well, don't worry, I'm going to find another boy to like this year. A cute one, such as David!

Me running down the driveway in my new blue shoes. Red skirt, swingy pleats, pretty! White blouse, short sleeves, pretty! White socks, rolled 2x. I am waving to Billy and Seymour, and they are sad and crying. They miss me a lot when I go to school. I miss them, too.

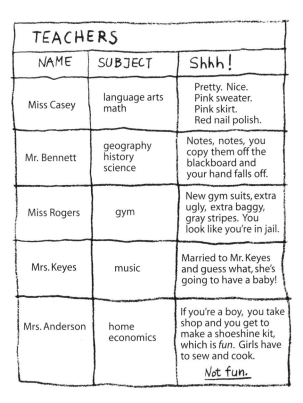

TEACHERS		
NAME	SUBJECT	Shhh!
Miss Casey	language arts math	Pretty. Nice. Pink sweater. Pink skirt. Red nail polish.
Mr. Bennett	geography history science	Notes, notes, you copy them off the blackboard and your hand falls off.
Miss Rogers	gym	New gym suits, extra ugly, extra baggy, gray stripes. You look like you're in jail.
Mrs. Keyes	music	Married to Mr. Keyes and guess what, she's going to have a baby!
Mrs. Anderson	home economics	If you're a boy, you take shop and you get to make a shoeshine kit, which is *fun*. Girls have to sew and cook. <u>Not fun.</u>

Poor little Seymour had an earache and he was crying and crying and it was the middle of the night and I went to the kitchen. Mama was cuddling sad Seymour and she was calling Dr. Mason in her bathrobe. I was trying to make Seymour laugh, but he wouldn't even play his favorite game, peekaboo. He just kept pulling his ear and crying so much. Then Billy woke up, and Sam was giving him a bottle, and now the whole family was there in the kitchen, and it was 2:00 in the morning! Then Dr. Mason was coming up the driveway with his fat black doctor bag. He looked in Seymour's ears and throat. Uh-oh, Seymour got a shot in his you-know-what, and he really cried, but after that he went to sleep, and so did I. Mama says I had the saddest earaches ever when I was a little baby. Poor little Katie!

Gotta go . . . school bus time . . . Wish me luck, Notebook . . . spelling test today. . . .

September 16, 1948

Dear Mrs. Leitstein,

Your letter was funny! I can picture your gray beret blowing off in the wind, whoooosh, and all those people chasing it for you, and the little boy who caught it. Sometimes, though, when I picture you walking alone in the city, I feel sad. I wish I could be walking with you.

   I am very mad at Miss Casey. She *used* to be my favorite teacher, but forget about that now! This is what happened: We got a new boy in our class. The principal brought him in at math time. Which is not my favorite time. I always sit there with my fingers crossed, praying Miss C won't call on me. The new boy's name is Rudy. He looked so scared. I feel sorry for anyone who has to be new. Last year it was me, that's what I said to Miss Casey. Well as soon as she heard that, *she made ME in charge of Rudy, booo!* The whole entire day, including *recess,* when all I wanted was to visit the 1st grade wing with Lucie. Sometimes 1st grade teachers let you read a story. So Joyce and Lara went with Lucie, and *they* all had a great time, while I was stuck with Rudy and his too-short pants, and now everyone thinks I like Rudy Pergolizzi. *Which I don't.* He used to live in Italy, and all the kids were laughing on account of his funny accent. Well, the new boy better find a friend tomorrow. Because I'm *not* (his friend). And that's why I'm mad at Miss Casey.

   Guess what, I made the swim team again! Our

bathing suits are green this year. Miss Mack says
if we practice hard, we could be the best in the
county. This girl called Maggie's on the team
again, too. We voted her captain. I like Maggie,
but I was hoping the girls would vote for me.

Yours truly,

Katie

Katie Roberts la crackerjack swimmer

PS: Do you like dogs, Mrs. L? I read a book about a
lady and her dog, and I thought of you. Because if
you had a dog, maybe you wouldn't be so lonely.

September 20, 5:30 P.M.

Katie Roberts, violin player!
There are four strings. And a bow.
You have to practice every day.
I can't wait to learn a song!

In music, everyone had to choose an instrument.
I was begging Lucie to take violin, like me, but
she picked clarinet. Then Joyce picked clarinet,
too. She is always copying Lucie. Now Lucie and
Miss Copy will march in the marching band, and
violin players aren't allowed. Which is a big
shame, because you get a special cap. And white

23

boots. Matthew is the class drummer—plug
your ears. David, the cutest boy on earth, picked
saxophone. Then Pamela, Miss Annoyance,
picked saxophone, and now *she* gets to sit next
to him twice a week in music. Why, why, why
didn't I pick saxophone?

*** Permission Slip ***

I give my child_____
permission to borrow a(n)_____
from the Meadowlawn School and return it in
excellent condition at the end of the school year.

September 21, 3:30 P.M.

Tonight when the sun goes down it will be
Yom Kippur. That's a big holiday if you're
Jewish, but you don't get presents. We're all
going to temple—even Billy and Seymour, and
they better not cry! Sam and Mama have to fast.
That means no food, not even a bite, for one
whole day. If I did that, my stomach would be
growling and grumbling and mad. Mama lights
a special candle for my father tonight, and she

says a special prayer. On Yom Kippur you have to *atone* for your sins. Sam was telling me how you have to be sorry about all the things you did that weren't nice this year. Well, I didn't have a lot of sins, maybe two teeny ones, that's it. I love wearing dress-up clothes to temple and sitting next to Mama, and she holds my hand. We look at all the people. When I was little, in NY, we walked to temple with my father Friday nights. Even if it was snowing outside! His coat was blue, and there were always little candies in the pocket.

Secret ! Sometimes in my tree house I make up a prayer. I just look at the sky and whisper. Yesterday I said one about no homework, but Mr. Bennett gave tons of it anyway.

Promise ! In honor of Yom Kippur, I, Katie Roberts, promise to be perfect all the time. I will not pout if I don't get my way. I will not have a messy room. Or leave dirty socks under the kitchen table. Or complain when Mama makes me go to boring old Hebrew school to learn all about being Jewish, even though I know everything already. Talk about Hebrew school, there's a new boy in my class and guess who it is? Rudy Pergolizzi, that's who. I bet his mother makes him go, too.

The Cupcakes
and the Mean Mother

by that famous child-author Katie Roberts

Once there was a girl. She had flowing blond hair
and two baby brothers and she loved them very
much and it was their 5-month birthday and she
wanted to make a surprise for the whole family.
Cupcakes! She worked and worked and a long
time later, 12 beautiful cupcakes were baking in
the oven. The girl went to her room to make a
Cute-Boys List. After that, she called her best
friend. They talked about boys. Then her mother
was yelling. "There's a big mess of flour and eggs
in my kitchen! Cupcakes are burning! What in the
world are you doing?!" The girl began to cry. All
she wanted was to make a wonderful surprise. A
nice mother would be proud not mad. Now there
were no cupcakes and the kitchen smelled bad. If
only she could run away with her brothers to
Alaska. They'd live in an igloo and eat cupcakes
every day. The Mean Mother would be sorry.
The End.

<u>September 30, 4:30 P.M.</u>

SUBJECT: FRENCH (*Bonjour! Bonjour!*)

Settle down, class, settle down! That's what
Mrs. Freeman says when she comes to room
202 to teach us French. She has pictures of
Paris. Lucie likes "Eiffel Tower" best. I like
"Outdoor Café" because there's a pretty French
girl and a boy drinking Coke. Whenever I look at
the picture, I turn bright red. I pretend I am the
girl. And David is the boy!

SUBJECT: HOME ECONOMICS

I hate sewing! I keep sticking myself with pins,
and all the stitches I make are crooked. Mrs.
Anderson won't let me sit next to Lucie anymore.
SHE says we talk too much. Which we don't. We
all have to make aprons for our mothers. Mine is
a mess so far.

SUBJECT: BOYS

David is sooo cute! Curly blond hair,
taller than me, and his blue shirt   DAVID   *David*
looks like sky. David, David! Like *me*   <u>DAVID</u>
instead of Pamela! Whenever he talks to that
snippy little snob, she is suddenly Miss Giggle
and Miss Charm. I told Lucie my secret about

liking D. Her eyes popped wide open. Why? Because a long time ago in 2nd grade she liked him, too! In 3rd grade she liked Luke.

The Famous Baby Song

Who loves babies?
Katie, Katie
Who loves babies
every day?

Katie loves big boys
Babies, babies
Katie loves babies
ya ha ha.

Who loves a Billy?
Who loves a Seymour?
Your big sister
that is who.

I love youuuuuu!

The Famous Baby Chart

Crawling	Yes	(No)	Sometimes
Clapping	Yes	No	Sometimes
Standing	Yes	(No)	Sometimes
Walking	Yes	(No)	Sometimes
Talking	Yes	No	Sometimes

(Ga-ga goo-goo! When Seymour talks, he looks in your eyes, like he's telling you a whole important story.)

October 14, 1948

Dear Mrs. Leitstein,

Guess what! Sam is buying a luncheonette and I'm allowed to help! It's all because Sam loves cooking so much. Of course, he loves our ranch, too, and all the cows, but sometimes, he says, you get tired of cows, you want to be with people. Tom Trimmer loves cows all the time, 100%, so Sam hired him to help around the ranch. Mr. Trimmer has one thumb instead of two. It got shot off in the war. Mama says it's rude to look at the place where his thumb should be, but I always do. I can't wait to start my job at our luncheonette, Mrs. L! It's at 21 Main Street, right across from the train station. The grand opening is soon. Maybe you can come! Sam reads millions of books from the library all about restaurants and recipes and cooking. Mama says we have to come up with a spunky name (for the luncheonette). Every night when we are eating dessert, we try and think up spunky names. By the way, Sam is teaching me his secret pancake recipe. It's a secret, but if you want, I can tell it to you. Today I tried making pancakes with blue-berries inside, but the berries got mushy, and the batter turned blue. What a big mess on the grid-dle. To cheer me up, Sam let me wear his special hat. It's from before the war, before this ranch, when he lived in NY like us, and he was in cooking school there. Sam's hat is the kind a real chef wears—it's tall and white and silly!

Thank you for sending me that old-time picture of you with your dog, Matilde. I can't believe that tiny girl is you! Sometimes when I see an old picture of me, I get a funny feeling inside. Because I used to be cute and I'm not anymore.

From your cooking pen pal,

Katie

Katie Roberts, future waitress

PS: Were you sad when Matilde died? I was sad when my father died. I wish I could see him again.

PPS: There's another word for pancakes, Sam told me. Flapjacks!

October 22, 7:00 P.M.

I went to Lucie's after school. Chocolate cake, good snack. When we were doing our amphibian reports, Joyce called Lucie, and they were talking for a long time, and I was mad. My report is 4 pages long: 3 diagrams, 1 chart. And Mr. Bennett better appreciate all this hard work. For my cover I made a picture of a frog jumping over another frog. Lucie says those are the funniest frogs she's ever seen. I hope Joyce's cover is ugly and I hope Lucie doesn't like Joyce too much.

SECRET: Do Not Tell! SECRET: Do Not Tell!

Lucie's sister (beautiful gorgeous perfect Jennie) wasn't home and we were looking in her dresser. Touch-of-Pink lipstick! Hair spray! Curlers! Coconut face cream! We tried everything. It was such a good time. Now the best, and it was under Jennie's pillow, shhh. A letter from a boy called Scott, wow! "Dear Jennie, I like you. Your friend Scott." I want a boyfriend sooo much, but who would ever like me? Too skinny, too tall, and I want to be pretty, like Jennie. I can't wait to be 14 like Jennie. I want a whole pile of secret letters. From David.

October 23, 7:15 P.M.

In science Mr. Bennett was talking all about
reptiles, yuck. He had pictures, and they made
me sick! I'm scared of reptiles, and especially
snakes. John in my class said he has a pet snake
5 feet long, then Eddie said it, too, and that really
made me sick, so I was plugging my ears. Then I
was doodling . . . city things, not snaky things . . .
3 tall buildings, 2 taxis, 1 trolley car. . . . And
that's when I thought up the best name for Sam's
luncheonette. THE TROLLEY CAR CAFÉ . . . !
I was so excited I forgot to be scared about the
reptiles. Sam and Mama say the Trolley Car
Café is the spunkiest name they've ever heard,

Yo ho ho

Every night I practice how to be a waitress,
which I am planning to be at the Trolley Car
Café. Billy and Seymour love playing restaurant
with me. I hold a tray high. "May I take your
order, Sirs? Today we have peach pie." They
laugh and clap. I have a pad, and a stubby
yellow pencil. I write fast . . . peach pie . . . milk.
I tap dance all around the bedroom. My brothers
think I'm a riot.

Sam and I painted a sign in the barn after
supper, and the cows were going moooo.
I like cows, especially Miss Paulette.
I don't like milking them, though,
it's too hard. But I'd rather milk
100 cows than do my report
on reptiles!

WELCOME TO THE TROLLEY CAR CAFÉ

Billy and his brand-new tooth.
One little tooth, sticking right up.
It's the cutest thing you've ever seen.

Sweetie-pie Seymour kissing himself in the mirror.

It's Mama's turn to host the monthly meeting
of the Langley Ladies' Book Club.
They drink tea and eat skinny little
sandwiches with their pinkies sticking
out. Talk, talk. I baby-sit Billy and
Seymour. Everyone notices.
Especially Matthew's mother.
Her stomach is big and round
because she's going to have a baby.
I hope she went home and said to
Mr. Pest Matthew, "That Katie Roberts
knows everything about taking
care of babies! What a great girl, wow!"

In language arts we are learning about poems.
Everyone has to write a poem about a house. I
wrote one about my old apartment house in
the city.

My House, by Katie

On Riverside Drive in a city
it was pretty
My house
had no mouse

When I read it out loud, Miss Casey didn't say
it was good, and I was mad. SHE says a poem
should make you *feel* something. SHE makes you
go back to your seat and try again. When your
poem gets good, it goes on the bulletin board. I
want mine on the bulletin board. Four are there
so far, and they aren't that wonderful. Except
Rudy's, his poem is kind of good. Which is
weird, because it doesn't even rhyme, and a lot
of the words are spelled wrong. It's about his
house in Italy.

HOUSE, by Rudy

Friday nite!
House on the hill
Mther cookd a speshl meel
    Fther came home erly
Hapy Friday nite!

Friday nite
House on the hill
Dark house
No one livs there now
Sad Friday nite

October 29, 9:30 P.M.

We miss Sam! We miss Sam! No fair, he's always at the luncheonette, all day, all night, getting everything ready for the grand opening. Tonight he wasn't coming home for supper again, and Mama said two times in a row, "This house is too quiet when Sam's not around," and that's when a great idea popped in my head. A night picnic, at the luncheonette! Mama, who *never* likes my ideas, sure liked this one. We put Billy and

Seymour in pajamas. We put potato salad and
fried chicken and cookies in a basket. Then we
drove to town to surprise Sam! Mama said, "Sit
down, Sam, you're working too hard." We put a
checkered blanket on the floor for the picnic,
and the babies jumped all over Sam, as usual.
Whenever he's around, they forget about me.
Which isn't very nice of Billy and Seymour, it
really hurts my feelings. We ate and ate and
there wasn't one crumb left. Then Sam was
showing us all around the kitchen. There's a
giant pancake griddle! Stacks of brand-new-
dishes! Silver mixing bowls! The biggest refriger-
ator in the world! Sam was showing us the menu
and it looked too plain, so I drew curlicues and
lots of hearts. Sam loves my fancy menu—he put
it on the wall. Millions of customers will see it!

My House in New York, by Katie (Roberts)

*My house
Was near the river*

*And I hate
Mashed potatoes and liver!*

Miss Casey says my poem needs more work.
I like my poem. Too bad, Miss Casey.

Mama went to Melinda's House of Beauty and
got a too-short haircut. Sam loves Mama's haircut. I don't. When we lived in New York, her
hair was long and fluffy. It was really pretty then.
While Mama was at Melinda's, I stayed home
with Billy and Seymour. Katie Roberts, champion
baby-sitter! We played fire engine, and I gave
them piggyback rides, and I pulled them all over
the yard in their red wagon, and I even showed
them my tree house. You could tell they wanted
to go up. Sorry, boys, this house is private.

I'm never getting my hair cut,
never again! All the girls in
7th grade have long hair,
and I want it, too. Mama's
always saying, "Katie, don't
follow the crowd." Well, I don't
follow the crowd. I just want
to look like everyone else,
what's so terrible about that?

November 3, 8:00 P.M.

Tomorrow is the grand opening of the Trolley
Car Café, and guess who's a big fat liar? Sam,
that's who. He promised I could have an

37

important job, but now some Marilyn person gets to be waitress, which is absolutely unfair. Mama's siding with Sam, as usual. "Don't be silly, Katie, children belong in school, not waiting on tables, Katie." Blah blah blah. And to think I used to like Sam. Well phooey to you, Mr. Liar.

Secret : I went to my tree house to be mad. I made up a prayer: Could You make sure no one comes to Sam's luncheonette?

November 4

The One-and-Only, Once-in-a-Lifetime GRAND OPENING of the Trolley Car Café

Picture # 1  Inside the Café

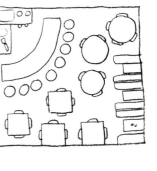

4 square tables
3 round tables
3 booths
1 curvy counter with 8 stools
that spin around

Picture # 2 Going to Town

That's me in the back seat with Billy and Seymour and I'm wearing dress-up clothes. Sam is driving the whole family to town. I'm still very mad about my job, but it's hard to stay mad at Sam. He's always singing in the car, and the windows are down, and after a while you're singing, too.

Picture # 3 Marilyn

Bright yellow hair. Short black skirt. Plays pat-a-cake with my babies, makes my babies laugh. I try not to like her, but she shakes my hand hard — "Hiya, Katie, looove your long hair!" — and gives me gum and shows me how to crackle when you chew. Which is fun, even though my mother gets mad.

Picture # 4 My Teeny Tiny Job

Sam says I can put salt in shakers and sugar in bowls. I do a good job. But I still want to be a real waitress with a special little pad. And a pencil behind my ear.

We waited for the big lunch crowd. We kept on waiting and no one came. Sam and Mama pretended to be cheery but you could tell they were sad, and it was all my fault. Why, why, why did I make up that stupid prayer about no customers, and how in the world can I erase it? The second we got home, I ran to my tree house and made up an emergency prayer: I really didn't mean that thing I said, and I'm sorry I said it, and I was wondering, if it isn't too much trouble, could You send a few customers to the Trolley Car Café tomorrow, please? It's over on Main Street, in case You forgot.

The Tall House, by Katie (Roberts)

Tall house in the city
snow!
Little feet
climbing stairs!
Warm up fast, dry your hair
It is long and pretty!

Miss Casey says she likes the little feet business, but my poem needs more heart. Whatever that means.

Personal and Private Letter to Miss Casey,
from Katie

Dear Miss Casey,
I love you, you are my favorite teacher on earth, and I think you should put my poem on the bulletin board immediately!

Very truly yours,

Katie Roberts, your biggest fan in room 202,
(and the girl who got 100% on two spelling tests in a row, ha!)

Will Katie give the letter to Miss Casey? Yes. No. Yes. NO. YES. (NO.)

November 8, 7:30 P.M.

I HATE SCHOOL!

Especially Mrs. Anderson and stupid, stupid
sewing. She sent a note to Mama. KATIE HAS
A BAD ATTITUDE. Wrong! Tomorrow she's
making me stay after, to fix the stupid pocket on
my stupid yellow apron. I was *supposed* to go to
Joyce's house with Lucie, so now it's the two of
them and I'm left out. Which I tried explaining
to Mama, but of course SHE'S on Mrs. A's side.
She never sides with me.

I hate SCHOOL!

Especially when Mrs. Keyes makes you play a
scale all by yourself in front of the class and your
violin is squeaking like crazy and you're trying
not to cry but tears fall down and you wish you
could sink through the floor.

I HATE school!

Especially when you're playing baseball at recess
and you miss the ball three times in a row and
your team loses and everyone thinks it's your
fault. And guess who's sitting on the bleachers
watching every single thing you do? Rudy. So
now he thinks I'm the worst baseball player in
Texas. Not that I care one little bit what he
thinks, so there.

I HATE SCHOOL!

Pamela's having a birthday party (with boys)
and she was giving out invitations in history.
First David, then Wendy, then lots of other kids.
I kept hoping I was next, but no luck. Lucie says
only girls who wear lipstick are invited. Lucie
wasn't (invited). Joyce was, even though she only
wore lipstick one time in art, and she borrowed
it from Lara. I told Joyce I don't care about
Pamela's dumb old party. What a big lie! Lucie
(no Joyce, ha!) came over after school. We drew
pictures of beautiful party dresses.

November 9, 3:30 P.M.

This is how you get invited to Pamela's party.
You wear lipstick! So . . . Lucie took her sister's
Touch-of-Pink to school . . . shhh! . . . I took
Mama's Paris Pink . . . shhh! . . . We put it on
in the girls' room and boy, were we shaking!
Because what if Miss Casey called our mothers!
Well, too bad for them. Because I felt pretty all
day, and so did Lucie. I looked mature, I hardly
looked like me. Here's the best: Everyone
noticed! Especially Wendy and Pamela! At lunch
they were smiling at me. See, they like you when
you wear lipstick, Lucie's right. And MY MOTHER

is wrong. This proves I have to wear it every day. Pamela, Pamela, say those magic words. . . . "Pleeease, Katie, please come to my party. I'll die if you say no!" Problem: All my dress-up clothes are way too babyish. I want a stylish black dress, the kind you see in magazines. Talk about babies, in homeroom Matthew said, "What's that goo on your face, Katie? You look weird." Matthew is so immature. Talk about boys, David has a new haircut. He looks extra cute. I want to dance with David! At Pamela's party!

November 14, 9:00 P.M.

We had a spelling bee in school. Boys against girls. "Photography . . . hippopotamus . . . " everyone was getting out but me! And David! All the girls were rooting for me and chanting my name, I felt so important. Go, Katie, Go! Spell, Katie, Spell! I wanted to win more than anything. I was standing across from David, and Miss Casey kept asking us to spell this word and that word, and this little song kept playing in my head.

David, David, I like David . . .
David, David, please like me . . .
Won't you carry, carry my books
and bring me chocolates!

I was so busy thinking how popular I'd be if David chose me for his girlfriend that I forgot about the two c's in occupation. Next thing you know, *David* is spelling bee champ, and all the boys are jumping around like the biggest bunch of babies and all the girls are moaning, even Lucie. I am very mad at David for winning that spelling bee, and for liking Pamela. He's not even that good a speller.

November 15, 8:30 P.M.

Pamela's party is right this very minute and I bet David is dancing with her right this very minute. I hate Pamela and all her stupid friends! I wish I could go to another school, far away from here. Just me and Lucie in a brand-new no-snob school. I am popular there. I have a boyfriend. He carries my books, and I go to millions of parties.

Me and Mama in my tree house. She is trying to cheer me up and we are eating pie and she's telling one of her famous stories. They're always about her when she was my age.

Mama's Story

7th grade!
That was the year
I was in love with the great
and wonderful Larry Barry.
At the school dance he asked
all the girls to dance, but
never me. I kept running to
the girls' room to cry. My
best friend, Louise, kept me
company there. Suddenly I
had an idea—I went back to
the gym and asked Larry to
dance. Well . . . he laughed at me.
So I stepped on his foot. Hard,
too, and the principal called my
parents, and I never spoke to that
horrid boy with the ridiculous
rhyming name ever again.

My mother's stories are silly. They cheer me up
a little.

November 30, 1948

Dear Mrs. Leitstein,

Get well soon! Feel better fast! I'm sorry you had a
cold and also a sore throat on Thanksgiving. Did
you eat chicken soup? We had turkey. Mama
always makes me chicken soup when I get a sore
throat. I get them a lot, and Dr. Mason says one of
these days my tonsils should come out. Does your
doctor say that, too? I like when Mama puts noo-
dles in the soup. They slide right down and then
you get better right away. I wish I could come over
to your house, Mrs. L. I'd bring soup on a tray.
Toast, too, and I'd read you my new story. After that
you'd dance around your house, and I would, too.

I miss you!

Katie

Katie Roberts, chicken soup girl

PS: Look in envelope! Here are two presents!
From me! For you!

Present #1

Babies Get a Haircut:
A Cheering-up Story
by Miss Katie Roberts,
your cheering-up pen pal

Sam says Billy and Seymour have too many curls,
and they look like girls. Uh-oh, Mama gets mad at
Sam. Then Sam gets mad at Mama, and it feels
like the whole world is mad. Sam stomps off to
the barn to milk cows. Mama stomps off with me
and the twins to the barber. Oh, brother! Whine,
whine, cry. Snip, cut. Wriggle, wriggle, squirm.
Snip, cut. Afterwards Mama is sad. "Oh dear, I'm
fighting with Sam and our babies don't look like
babies anymore!" When we get home, Sam is sitting on the fence with a flower for Mama, and
that's the end of the fighting, and now everything
is back to normal. Except Billy and Seymour have
no curls. But don't worry, they still look like babies!

The End.

Present #2

Your ticket, Oooohh-la-la!

> You are cordially invited to lunch at
> # THE TROLLEY CAR CAFÉ
> 21 Main Street
> Langley, Texsas

PPS: I hope you like the name of our luncheonette, Mrs. Leitstein, because I'm the one who thought it up! You can sit at the counter when you come. That's where I sit, and Sam makes chocolate shakes and grilled-cheese sandwiches and they are sooo good. But it's sad when no one's there except one old man and me. Sam likes talking to that man about everything in the world. He's new in town, and his sewing shop is new on Main Street, and one time I saw him in temple. He was sitting next to Rudy from my class. Well, I hope all the tables get filled up soon so Mama quits worrying so much. Sam says, "Rome wasn't built in a day. Filling up your luncheonette takes time." He's always looking on the bright side. Mama says she loves that about Sam. I get a funny feeling inside when Mama says she loves Sam. Because what about my father? Okay, from now on, I'm going to look on the bright side, too. Every single minute.

<u>*December 1, 4:00 P.M.*</u>

No fair! No fair! No fair! Miss Casey made *me* the spelling tutor of Rudy. Which means I have to miss recess every single Tuesday and Friday until he learns to spell. Which could take forever.

Hanukkah Pictures,
by Katie Roberts, girl-artist

This watch used to be my father's. It is big and round with a new green strap, and a long time ago he taught me to tell time on it. Mama's been keeping it just for me. For Hanukkah she wrapped it with pink ribbon for a surprise. When I put it on, I was all mixed up happy and sad thinking, "Hello, Daddy, it's me, your little girl, Katie, only I'm not that little anymore, and I wish, wish, wish you were coming up the road with your duffel right now. . . . I'd run outside—the screen door would slam—and then I'd be hugging you forever! I love my watch so much. And my father.

Potato pancakes. Mama's are so good, you eat until your buttons pop!

The No-Nap Babies. I made a whole entire book for Billy and Seymour for Hanukkah—wow, what a sister! I put curly lambs on the cover and a dedication inside, like the kind you see in real books: "For my favorite no-nap boys, Billy & Seymour."

It's my turn to light the candles, and Sam tells the Hanukkah story. Outside, it's scary black night, and you can hear the wind in the leaves in the trees, but here in the kitchen, we are extra cozy. "Hanukkah oh, Hanukkah, come light the menorah..." (Hebrew school song)

December 9, 9:30 P.M.

I was reading in bed, all snuggly and cozy and warm, a medium-good book about Betsy Ross. She made the first American flag, la-di-da, what a girl, I bet *her* sewing teacher loved Betsy. Anyway, I got thirsty and I was going to get water and I wasn't wearing slippers, so the floor didn't creak too much which is why Mama and Sam didn't hear me coming. They were talking in low voices in the kitchen. Serious grownup talk. Worried talk. About too-big bills and too-little money and too-few customers at the Trolley Car Café. I wasn't thirsty anymore and I felt sad all over because I love our luncheonette so much, and why don't people want to go there? Poor Sam, I bet his feelings are hurt. He must think people don't like his cooking, but he's a great cook, better than all the cooks in Langley. He even knows how to make string beans taste good. And one more thing. What if we run out of money?

December 9, 9:30 P.M.

Boys, Boys, Oh, My Troubles with Boys

Rudy: Everyone else is outside having fun at recess and I'm stuck with Rudy the Silent in the back of the school library. Miss Casey gave me a spelling list. Easy words from 2nd grade.

happy   parrot tugboat
Texas   airplane garage

It is so boring when I'm sitting there with Rudy. He doesn't talk to me. He just spells if I tell him to, and mostly he spells wrong. But after I say "h-a-p-p-y, h-a-p-p-y" a lot of times, he finally gets it right. G-r-u-m-p-y, g-r-u-m-p-y R-u-d-y.

Matthew: I was playing blocks with Billy and Seymour. We were building a tall building, and that's when Mama called, "Katie, there's a boy on the phone!" Whoa, those blocks came falling down, and I was tripping on my own big feet . . . running to the phone, praying it would be David. But it was only Matthew. "I got a puppy," he said, "and also a baby sister, called Jamie." M said, "Katie, how do you stand all that crying all night?" I said, "Plug your ears; it's the only thing that works." He kept talking, about baseball—

what else?—and his hero, Mr. DiMaggio—who else?—and now there's a second hero, too, Mr. Jackie Robinson. I like that name. When I have a baby one day, if it's a boy baby, I'm calling him Jackie Robinson.

December 23, 9:00 P.M.

Mama said, "Has anyone seen my lipstick?" "Not me," I said. My heart was pounding away. Paris Pink! I took it to school this morning so I could be pretty for Christmas Assembly. But stupid me forgot to put it back in her drawer, and now I'd lied to Mama. I was so scared about putting it back because what if she caught me putting it back? Finally, when Mama was taking a bath, I ran to her room and left the lipstick in exactly the right spot. I ran out fast. No one saw.

December 28, 7:10 P.M.

Christmas vacation! No homework for 10 whole days! Except, I'm still trying to write a great poem. It's going to be a surprise for Miss Casey. We finished the poetry chapter, but I'm hoping if I ever write a good one, she'll put it on the bulletin board. (But NOT next to Pamela's poem, the most boring thing on earth.) Every morning after breakfast I try and write a poem that doesn't rhyme too much. I sit on the kitchen floor, against the cupboard. I wear red socks. Poem-writing socks. Billy and Seymour try and snatch my pencil. They crawl all over me until I pay attention to them. I say, "Okay, boys, now I will teach you how to talk." We play school, but they won't sit still.

My poem-writing socks

Me: *Say, Katie!*
Babies: MAMA, MAMA, MAMA.
Me: *Say, Katie!*
Babies: DADA, DADA, DADA.

I wish they'd say my name. Mama promises they'll say every single thing, and especially Katie, in their own good time.

Lucie came over today, and we had a picnic. It was cold in the tree house, and we shared my gray gloves. It was fun. We made bead bracelets with Lucie's Christmas bracelet kit. 18 beads make a bracelet. Joyce came, too, after her dancing lesson, and the picnic wasn't that much fun anymore. I hate the way she's always hogging Lucie.

January 4, 1949

Dear Mrs. Leitstein,

A long time ago when you were in 7th grade, did a boy ever ask you to dance? I've never gone to a dance before, but we're having one at school. Valentine's Day, and everybody goes. Lucie's sister Jennie, who used to be in 7th grade, says you wear a fancy dress and stockings, not socks. Lipstick! Satin shoes! You go to the beauty parlor! Lucie's kind of scared about the dance. I am, too, a little.

Today I read a story to the cutest 1st graders in the world! I know you're not supposed to have favorites, but I do: Mary Helen Peters, and she's got this stubby little braid with the ends coming out, and her hair is streaky blond like mine. Her skirt is plaid with pleats. If I had a little sister, I wish she could be Mary Helen Peters.

Remember Rudy, the boy in my class who used to live in Italy? Well, Miss Casey picked *me* to be his spelling tutor! It's a very important job, Mrs. Leitstein. Only, some of the boys — and also some girls, like Big Snob Pamela and Big Snob Wendy — say mean things to me, like "Ooohhh, someone likes Rudy!" Then I get mad at Rudy. Because it's all his fault for being a rotten speller. But you know what's weird? Sometimes I feel sorry for Rudy. No friends. See, he hardly talks and never smiles, and he doesn't play baseball at recess. He just sits by himself on the bleachers, drawing pictures or staring at the sky. Mama says he must be awfully shy. I used to be shy and I still am sometimes. Especially around cute boys, and there's a really cute one in my class, called David. If you ask me, Rudy better start playing baseball and acting crazy at lunch like all the boys. Because that's what you do in Texas—you follow the crowd. Then you have friends.

From your friendly pen pal!

Katie

Katie Roberts

.

January 7, 7:00 P.M.

Miss Mack says winning isn't everything. Which is crazy. Because who wants to lose a swim meet? And who wants to lose two in a row? Not me! Afterward we go to the home ec room for a snack. What a surprise: Mrs. Anderson tries being nice. She has cookies and milk for the home team (us) and for the visiting team (Bowling Green School), and you almost forget she gave you a 70% on your apron, even though you tried and tried to do a good job. I sit next to Frances. We whisper about Mrs. A! I like Frances, but of course I like Lucie much better.

Here I am kicking very hard and pulling with all my might, but I can't keep up with Gail, Miss Speed from the Bowling Green team. Boy, she makes me mad. So does MY MOTHER. I keep looking at the bleachers where she always sits, but she's not there. Why? Because Billy banged his thumb in a drawer, and of course Billy's thumb is way more important than my swim meet. Sam isn't there either. He has to be at the Café. In case some people on Main Street get hungry.

ANNOYING BOSSY MOTHER EXAMPLE #4

The minute you're on the phone with Lucie after a hard day at school, she thinks up something else for you to do. Like practice violin. Which is not your favorite thing to do. But off you go to your room to play "Pony Waltz" five times in a row. Is the Bossy Mother happy? Of course not, and here comes a lecture . . . ."Will you shut that door, Katie, the babies are napping, Katie, and you're waking them up with that song!"

January 14, 6:15 P.M.

Subject: TELEPHONE.

The black one on the wall in the kitchen. I want it to ring! Now! Today! Right this very minute! I want it to be some extra-cute high school boy, whoa! His name can be Theodore and he likes me like crazy and he's mature. Too bad, baby David, because why would I like you? Theodore writes mushy letters every day, and I keep them under my pillow. I get chocolates, too, and he carries my books in school. Everyone notices.

SUBJECT: BOYS

Billy and Seymour needed shoes. In the shoe store I was in charge of Seymour. Mama had Billy. Seymour kept sliding off my lap, and when I was chasing him under the counter, guess who came into the store? Matthew. I felt so stupid because stupid Matthew saw me crawling on the floor. His mother was holding their new baby. Boy, is she cute. Way cuter than Matthew! Then Mama sent me next door to buy two blue zippers at the sewing shop and I tripped on the step going in, and who was there in the shop watching me trip? Rudy. I bought the zippers fast and left fast. After that, Mama and I took the babies down the street to the Trolley Car Café. Sam made a big fuss about their new shoes, and so did Marilyn. No one paid attention to me.

Shoes make Seymour mad. No matter how many times you tie up the laces, he pulls and pulls until they come off.

Billy loves his shoes so much. He cries when you take them off at nap time, and he's always bending down to pat them, like he's patting his yellow bunny.

January 14, 6:15 P.M.

Sometimes when I am tutoring Rudy, I pretend I
am his teacher! I made a special RUDY folder. I
carry it under my arm to the library. Joyce loves
my folder and now she's dying to help me tutor
Rudy. What a brat. She's always trying to steal
Lucie, and now Rudy. Miss Casey sometimes
gives a pop quiz. Today I gave Rudy a pop quiz.
He got three right and three wrong. "That's too
many wrong," I told Rudy. "If you want to be a
good speller—like me, you'd better study harder."
What a bad sport! He walked right out of the
library. Good riddance, Rudy, you have a bad
attitude! I packed up my folder. But I was scared
about what to tell Miss Casey. What if she got
mad at me? So I looked all over until I finally
found Rudy in the art room. "Fine," I said, "no
more pop quizzes." Then I followed him back
to the library. Back to work.

| tired | cowboy | baseball |
| challenge | friendship | Mississippi |

January 21, 8:28 P.M.

Sam and Mama have this **VERY PRIVATE** book
and I'm not allowed to look inside because it's all
about money, and every week they put the book

on the kitchen table and look inside and add
and subtract and whisper. I pretend to write in
my notebook. I pretend to do my homework. I
pretend I don't hear when they say that the
Trolley Car Café is gobbling up their savings.
Tonight Sam said, "I love the café, but maybe I'd
better go back to the cows full time. We sure do
need the money." Then Mama gave Sam a big
lecture! Don't give up, don't be a quitter, Sam. . . .
We'll figure out something together. . . . I was
glad Mama wasn't lecturing me this time, but I
felt sorry for Sam. Maybe I'll give him some
money??? I have $9.42 in a glass jar on my
desk, my whole entire life savings. Okay,
tomorrow I'm giving Sam $2.00,
aren't I wonderful!

TOTAL
$9.42

January 24, 10:15 P.M.

    Concert!
    You Are Cordially Invited
    Thursday at 5:00 P.M.
    Meadowlawn School
    Refreshments

Meadowlawn Orchestra

For days and weeks I've been shaking and
scared. All because of Mrs. Keyes and her bad
ideas. Bad idea #1 Concert. Bad idea #2 Practice,

practice, practice, until you're sick of every song. Bad idea #3 She picked *me* for a violin solo. I have to play "Springtime" in front of millions of people! Including David! And Mama, Sam, and the twins! Two things happened—Tommy forgot his trumpet, and Lara had a stomachache and wouldn't come out of the girls' room—so the concert started a whole hour late. Wendy, of all people, got to be announcer . . . "Ladies and gentlemen, children of all ages, introducing . . . the Meadowlawn Orchestra. . . ." Bravo, bravo! *I* wanted to be announcer, but of course *I* never get picked for the good jobs. Mrs. Keyes was waving her baton, and her stomach was giant, on account of being pregnant, and we played "Swanee River." Then Matthew played drums, and everyone loved Matthew. They were clapping forever. Then it was my turn, help! My legs were 1,000 pounds of jelly, and my arms, too. I wanted to run off the stage. Then . . . Mrs. Keyes was running off the stage! To have her baby! Everything went crazy, and kids were jumping around yelling, "Yippiaa," and Mr. and Mrs. Keyes were on their way to the hospital with everyone waving from windows. Well, that was the end of the concert. Ho ho ho, no solo for Katie! Thank you, baby Keyes!

Yippiaa !!

10:35 P.M. P.S. Someone just called Mama. It's a girl, and her name is Lily. I bet she's so cute.

Miss Lily Keyes

January 28, 5:30 P.M.

Mama's making me a new dress for the Valentine's Dance. We went to the sewing shop to pick fabric. Well guess who was working behind the counter? Rudy, that's who. He knows how to use the cash register. What a big showoff. I pretended not to notice, I did not talk to Rudy. Mama talked to the *nice* person behind the counter, the very nice person Mr. Pergolizzi. He is Rudy's grampa. Rudy's lucky. He gets to use a cash register *and* he's got a grampa. My grampas died before I was born, and so did my grandmas, which is totally not fair because whenever I read a book and there's a grandma in that book, she is always extra nice and she always sides with the child. Mr. P was talking all about Sam (he likes Sam!) and the Trolley Car Café (he likes our café) and a city called Rome, and Mama was touching all the fabrics and talking, too,

for a long time. She's always being friendly
and making new friends, it's so embarrassing.

This is how I want my dress to look.
Long and black and mature. Of course,
she says, "That's inappropriate, Katie,"
and gets her way again. And I get to look
like a baby again, in a powder blue dress
that's way too short. I'll never have a
good time in a dress like that. Or maybe
I just won't go to the dance.

Mr. Pergolizzi used to live in Italy, like Rudy, and
Mama says he's sweet as pie. I wish I had a grampa
with white hair, and a fuzzy white mustache.

February 7, 4:45 P.M.

In history we are learning about cities. Everyone
has to pick a city and write a big report, and you
need a partner for your report. The second Mr.
Bennett said the word "partner," that RAT Joyce
grabbed Lucie and that was the end of me. I'm
never speaking to Joyce again, that's all there is
to it. Everyone was asking everyone, "Will you be
my partner? . . . Will you be my partner?" And I
wanted to ask David, but what if he said no? Or
laughed at me? Before you know it, every single

person had a partner but me. And Rudy. So who's got Rudy again? Me again. Which is totally 100% unfair. I told Mr. Bennett I could only write a report with a girl partner. He said lots of girls were working with boys, for example, David and Gloria. Well, la-di-da for them.

We were all squeezing next to the big map to pick a city, and Matthew screamed, "I call New York!" I told Mr. Bennett I should have NY, since I used to live there. But of course Matthew got his way since he asked first. What a big baby! So now I have Rudy *and* Minneapolis, and it's the hardest word to spell, even if you know how to spell hard words in the first place. Lucie's doing Phoenix. With Rat.

I gave a note to Lucie in art.

Dear Lucie,
Are we still best friends?
Yours truly,
Katie Roberts

Here's Lucie's poem. Which she gave me in gym.

Roses are red
Violets are blue
We'll always be best friends
True, true, true!

February 8, 9:30 P.M.

> # TROLLEY CAR CAFÉ!
> GOOD FOOD AT GOOD PRICES
> *specializing in pancakes*
>
> **GOOD SERVICE**
> **CONGENIAL ATMOSPHERE**
>
> CHILDREN OF ALL AGES WELCOME

Sam and Mama are putting an advertisement in the Langley Times on page 1, where everyone can see it! Guess who thought up the line about CHILDREN OF ALL AGES WELCOME. Me, Katie Roberts! We drove to town with our ad, and I got to bring it inside, with $2.50 for the editor. He wore a little cap, and the sign on his desk said EDITOR and it was the biggest desk in the world. When I grow up, the first thing I'm going to be is a writer of important books. After that, I might get a job at the *Langley Times*. I'll have my very own typewriter, of course, and a great big desk. And a boyfriend!

<u>February 10, 8:55 P.M.</u>

Boys

Rudy: Spelling test, and he gets 80%! Which is way better than the last test, which was only 68. Miss Casey wrote, "Good Work, Rudy," across the top of his paper. Rudy, Mr. No-Smile, was practically smiling when he saw 80.

Matthew: Three nights in a row at exactly 7:00 the telephone rings, and three nights in a row it's Matthew. Le Pain. He talks and talks . . . about his puppy, Fluffy, and his precious new picture of Jackie Robinson. I hang up fast. Mama says I'm rude, but I have better things to do than listen to Matthew blab away. Mostly, I have to practice dancing in front of the bathroom mirror! Four days 'til the Valentine's dance, yikes! Lucie says if a boy calls three times in a row, he definitely likes you. Well, Matthew better NOT like me, because I like David.

David: I typed a letter to David. Lucie says it's a really good letter.

> Dear David,
>
> If you want, I will dance with you
> at the Valentine's Dance.
>
> From, Katie

Will Katie mail the letter?   YES. No. yes. (NO.)

$\mathcal{February}$ 12, 9:22 P.M.

Rudy's apartment is right upstairs from the
sewing shop. I went there after school. The
kitchen table is yellow! We worked on our city
report. Minneapolis is way far away from Texas.
Maybe I'll go there one day, because it snows a
lot there, and I really like snowstorms, snowmen,
and blizzards. I wish it would snow for once in
Langley. It's like they forget about winter here.
Rudy's mother wasn't home. It was too quiet in
that house. A cake was on the counter, and pictures by Rudy were everywhere. Rudy's always
doodling in his notebooks, like me. Mrs. Reidy,
the art teacher, loves telling him how great he is.
. . . "You really have a talent, Rudy. . . .
Wonderful pictures, Rudy. . . ." Which she used
to tell me. Well, I wanted to work on the cover,
but Rudy said I had to look up population,
recreation, and natural resources. Then he was
painting a map and it looked so real, like the
kind you get at the gas station. We ate the whole
cake except one little square, and I was making
up a cheerleading song . . . "Give me an Min . . .
nea . . .polis. . . ." It was fun. You could hear
Rudy's grampa coming slowly up the stairs. He
said, "Good evening, Katie," and patted my hand
in a very nice way. His mustache goes up when

he smiles. He said, "Next time, you have dinner."
Whoa! Imagine me at a boy's house for dinner!

Secret! Here's a teeny tiny secret for my notebook.
Rudy is a tiny little, teeny little, teeny little bit cute . . .
shhh . . . curly black hair, black-brown eyes. . . .
I can't tell anyone. Not even Lucie.

February 14

The First and Last Valentine's Dance of Katie Roberts

All Pictures by Katie Roberts

Picture #1 **THE DRESS**
I don't look like me in my new blue dress.
I look like some other Katie, some awfully grown-up
Katie. I begged and begged and finally Mama said
yes to silk stockings. But no lipstick, booo. I called Lucie and
Lucie called Joyce and Joyce said I could borrow hers at the
dance. Maybe J isn't so bad, after all.

Picture #2 **THE HAIR**
Sam drives me over and my stomach is
knots and I keep fixing my hair. Left part.
Right part. Bangs flat. Bangs fluffy. No part.
Sam talks a lot. About my mother, the twins, the
Trolley Car Café. (14 people for breakfast today, 18 for lunch,
hurray! Sam says it's all because of the ad. I want the whole
world to be in love with our café!) In the car Sam says, "You
look quite pretty tonight, Miss Roberts, quite mature." Sam's
nice. Most of the time, not all of the time. No grownup is
nice all the time, ha!

Picture #3 THE PUNCH BOWL

Paper hearts all over the gym, and music! Teachers in dress-up clothes! Boys in ties, grabbing cookies! Lucie and I and Maggie and Joyce stay near the punch bowl. We all touch Joyce's beauty-parlor hair. Paul asks Joyce to dance. Todd asks Lucie. Eddie asks Maggie, and no one asks me. I think a little prayer: please let me sink through the floor.

Picture #4 THE GIRLS' ROOM

David is dancing with Emily, not me. David is dancing with Annie, not me, then Frances. Tommy and Matthew are pouring punch and punching each other on the arm, and punch spills on my dress. Matthew asks me to dance. NO! Then Rudy asks and I say I have a sore toe and he acts like I'm a big liar. Too bad, Rudy! Just because we do a report together doesn't mean we have to dance together. I only want to dance with David. When will David like me? I run to the girls' room and stand there looking at my stupid red lips in the stupid ugly mirror. I wash my lips hard, and the whole world tastes like soap.

Picture #5 THE MOTHER

I call Mama from the nurse's office and she picks me up early, and I curl up in the front seat all the way home. She hugs me at the red light. I'm *never* going to another dance for the rest of my life.

The End.

February 16, 4:30 P.M.

I heard the worst thing today. It's about Rudy. This is what happened. We were in the library making a table of contents for our report, and I was still mad at Rudy for asking me to dance, and because all the pictures he made about Minneapolis were better than mine. Rudy kept staring at my watch. You could tell he liked it a lot. I was bragging how it used to be my father's. He was a very brave soldier, I said, and a long time ago he died in the war. Then this secret came tumbling out of me, I don't know why:

 Sometimes I think about my father three days in a row. Other times a whole week goes by and I don't think about him at all, and then I feel bad.

I felt so stupid telling that to Rudy. . . . Then all of a sudden he was telling me the saddest story in the world. Which is this: Rudy's parents died in the war, both of them, and also his grandma. And once he had a little sister, and she was 6, with a special toy lamb, and she died, too. When I heard that, I started to cry.

At lunch I *had* to be alone for once with Lucie, and I yelled at Joyce, and she said I could never use her lipstick again. I whispered to Lucie for a long time about Rudy. Lucie said if both her parents died, she'd be crying every second for the rest of her life.

After school I didn't want a snack. I didn't play with Billy and Seymour. I went straight to my tree house, which is where I am right now. I want to be alone, but I feel too lonely.

1:30 A.M. (Middle of the Night)

Mama is sitting on my bed and I am shivering like a big baby with a bad dream. We turn on the lamp and talk about Rudy. How he's Jewish like us. How so many Jewish people died in Europe in the war, just for being Jewish. It's so sad, I keep saying that to Mama, and she cries, too. At least Rudy's safe, she says, and Mr. Pergolizzi. She tucks the blanket under my feet like a nest, to warm my toes. I bet Rudy's little sister had curly black hair. I wish she were here with us now. Safe and sound in Texas.

KATIE'S HOW TO BE A PERFECT CHILD LIST

** because from now on, she's going to be perfect every second of her life **

1. Do all chores before Mama tells you to.

2. Be extra nice to Rudy, and say hi even if someone like Wendy is watching. Even if Tommy and Paul laugh at you. Even if the whole class starts singing, "Katie likes Rudy."

3. "Get that hair out of your eyes, Katie!" When Mama says that 10x in a row, go straight to your room and brush it back in a neat ponytail. Even if you look like 7 again.

4. Be extra nice to Rudy when you're helping him with spelling. Tell him he has a good attitude.

5. Don't go, "Ha-ha" when you swim faster than Maggie at practice.

6. Be extra nice to Rudy when you are working on your city report. Tell him 2x, or maybe 4x, "Hey your pictures are great."

7. When you ask Sam 5x in a row, "Can I work at the café, pleeeease," and he says 5x in a row, "Not today Katie," don't go slamming doors.

February 18, 1949

Dear Mrs. Leitstein,

At the Valentine's Dance, Mrs. Owens, the principal, was guarding the cookies! She was yelling at boys who were taking too many!

Remember I'm the spelling tutor of Rudy? Well, yesterday we had a spelling test and he got 90%! Which is a really great mark for Rudy. Miss Casey wrote a letter to me! On pink stationery!

Dear Katie,
Thank you for helping Rudy. I am proud of Rudy and I'm very proud of you.
Gratefully yours, Miss Casey

Rudy speaks Italian, did I tell you that already? He used to live in Rome. After that, England, and after that he moved to Texas, like me. In Rome, when you say *buon giorno,* it means "hello." Rudy's parents died in the war. All the people in his family died; there's nobody left except Rudy and his grampa. Isn't that the saddest thing you've ever heard? They live over the sewing shop on Main Street, just the two of them. There's a tiny flower garden out back. Every morning, Mr. Pergolizzi cuts a flower to put on their kitchen table. In a glass filled halfway with water. You would like Rudy's grampa, Mrs. Leitstein. He's old like you and really nice like you!

In art we have new paints, and I am painting a picture for you, so look for a surprise in your mailbox. It will be there soon! It's you and me on a green bench in the city, and our mittens are red, and it's snowing like a blizzard. We are eating pie. I'm putting my personal autograph on the picture! "To Mrs. Leitstein, my great pen pal. Love, Katie Roberts."

Now I have something to tell you. It's about me. Sometimes I'm not that nice. At the school dance, Matthew, who is such a big baby, asked me to dance and I said no, and I think I hurt his feelings. It's not that Matthew's a terrible person or anything. To tell you the truth, he's even fun sometimes. I like when he talks about his dog. Also, I didn't dance with Rudy. Oh, and sometimes I borrow Mama's lipstick and forget to tell her. And something else. Once when Joyce wasn't looking, I put her sneakers under the bleachers, and the gym teacher put an X in her attendance book because Joyce wasn't prepared for gym that day. Well, I wanted you to know. I hope you still like me. Because I like you and love you. If I had a grandma, Mrs. Leitstein, I would want her to be you.

From your trying-to-be-good pen pal,

Katie

Katie Roberts

February 23, 5:30 P.M.

Billy and Seymour love our cows. Because I'm such a wonderful sister, ha, I take them out to the barn when I'm tired of doing homework. We talk to the hired man, Tom Trimmer, who sings songs about cows and tells good cowboy stories. Today Billy was rolling in hay getting hay in his hair, and Seymour was looking in my pocket for a cookie. I said, "Seymour, I'll give you a cookie if you say my name." He was mad.

Say, Katie
COOKIE !
Say, Katie
COOKIE !
Say, Katie
KATIE !

I was so excited, I gave him two cookies! I gave Billy one, too, even though he never did say my name. Not even once.

IMPORTANT LETTER. To _David_. From _Katie_.

Dear David,

I saw you playing baseball when I was in the library. You hit the ball far, and when Tommy caught it I was mad, because then you were out. Don't worry, you're still a good player. I know a lot about baseball, so if you have any questions, ask me.

From,
Katie Roberts

The first letter I wrote to David is still in my tree house. Will Katie mail letter #2?

Yes. No. Yes. (NO.)

The Working Girl

by that incredibly hard-working author
Katie Roberts

Once there was a girl and she was mature. She
knew a lot of French words and she could swim
16 laps without stopping once, and she knew all
about how to be a waitress. But they NEVER let
her work in the café on Main Street. Why? Because
her MOTHER said, "Children belong in school!"
Well, one Sunday afternoon, Marilyn the waitress
had a great big sneezing kind of cold, and she was
coughing, too, and she had a fever. Good news,
the girl could be waitress that day! At 1:30, six
people came into the café. They said, "What's
good here?" The working girl said, "The pancakes
are très bien." They said, "Pancakes are for breakfast." The working girl said, "Sam's are très bien
any old time—you should try the ones with blue-
berries." Mmm, they all loved and adored those
pancakes. There wasn't one speck left, not even a
dot of maple syrup! Then something happened.
The working girl dropped a pitcher, splat. Orange
juice flew everywhere and what a big mess. The
mop was too heavy, and she started to cry because
she's too clumsy and because everyone was laughing at her. Then the bell over the front door jin-
gled, and a little 1st grader with fat braids came

into the café. Mary Helen Peters! The working
girl said, "Hello, Mary Helen," in her mature
voice. You could tell the little one was impressed.
This working girl read to 1st graders *and* worked
in a café! At the end of the day, Sam gave the
working girl $2.00. That night she was so
tired, she went to bed without supper.
The End

February 27, 4:00 P.M.

In history Matthew was reading his report (with
Emily) about New York City, and it wasn't that
good because every other word was something
to do with the Yankees in the Bronx and the
Dodgers in Brooklyn. I liked Emily's picture of
the Empire State Building. I went there once, a

long time ago, with Mama. At the end, Matthew said, "Katie Roberts used to live in NY, and she talked about it so much, you'd think you were practically there, and that's why I chose New York." Everyone was staring at me and I was bright, blushing, disgusting red. Ooohh, I hated Matthew. He's NOT allowed to be talking about me in front of the whole class.

Then Lucie and Joyce told everything in the world about Phoenix. They were giggling away, having a fine old time. I hope Mr. Bennett didn't think their report was wonderful. Because it wasn't.

Then it was Minneapolis time. I did the reading. Rudy showed his pictures, and he forgot to show mine. A lot of the kids kept asking Rudy, "Did you really draw that, really by yourself?" and no one was asking me anything. When it was over, I sat down fast, but not Rudy. Mr. Bigshot. Mr. Showoff. At recess, Matthew was showing Rudy that crumpled picture of Joe DiMaggio. Which made me feel crummy inside, I don't know why.

ANNOYING BOSSY MOTHER EXAMPLE #5
She decides to invite Mr. Pergolizzi to lunch next Sunday. Rudy, too. NO, NO, NO boys for lunch, help!

<u>March 4, 9:30 P.M.</u>

COMPANY FOR LUNCH

All artwork by Katie

Picture #1 *The Flower*
Mr. Pergolizzi brings a flower from his garden
for Mama. She acts like it's the most gorgeous
thing she's ever seen.

Picture #2 *Hamburgers and Macarony Salad*
At lunch the grownups do all the talking. They can
make me sit next to Rudy, but they cannot make me
talk to him. Billy and Seymour keep standing
in their highchairs. They won't pay
attention to anything I say.

Picture #3 *Sam's Bad Idea*
Sam: How about showing Rudy your tree house!
Me: My tree house is private.
Mama: Katie, how unkind!

Picture #4 *Mind Your Own Business!*
Rudy's in my tree house, and you can tell
he loves it a lot. Oh no, my letters for David
are on my big pillow and Rudy's looking at my
letters! "Mind your own business!" I scream.
"You don't know anything and you have no
friends, and I wish you never came here!"
Then Rudy's eyes are all filled up like big
brown pools, and I'm the meanest
girl in Texas.

PRIVATE
PRIVATE

March 6, 4:00 P.M.

I was trying to tutor Rudy. Because I know about
being responsible. Not because I care one bit
about him and his millions of spelling mistakes.
He was drawing the whole time, and he wouldn't
do one thing I said. Rudy the Silent. Rudy who
reads your private letters, then gets mad at *you*.

The Lipstick and the Mean Mother

a sad tale by Katie

Once there was a girl and she was in a bad
mood, so she borrowed her mother's lipstick.
Ravishing Red, my, my! Which she saved to put on
at school. Which wasn't a terrible thing to do. Lots
of girls wore lipstick, why shouldn't she? Anyway,
that day, the girl forgot her lunch, so Mother drove
it to school. Uh-oh, big shock, lipstick on her girl.
In the afternoon, the girl got off the school bus
and slowly walked up the road. Her head was
down. Her shoulders were not back. The Mean
Mother was waiting on the front porch. "You, sit
down!" she said. The girl sat on a wicker chair.
"It's the sneaking around I don't like," Mother
said, "and that color is too dark." The girl began
to cry. Because her mother thought she looked

stupid and because she did look stupid and because she was a bad person. When the crying was over, they drank lemonade. After a while, Mother said, "Maybe a lighter color would be okay, for special occasions only." The girl felt happy and unhappy at the same time. It was too confusing. She put the lipstick in her mother's top drawer, then went to her room to be moody for the rest of her life.
The End.

Ravishing Red

March 9, 12:30 P.M.

I am sitting on the bleachers all by myself and it's recess. Lucie is marching across the field with the marching band and her clarinet and her new white boots. I'm supposed to be tutoring Rudy, but he didn't come to the library. Ever since he went snooping around my tree house, he acts like *I'm* the worst person in the world. Look at him now, sitting way far away on the other side of the bleachers drawing pictures in a pad, instead of writing spelling words 10x each.

See if I care, Rudy Pergolizzi! Be my guest, fail
your spelling tests, see if I care!

March 9, 10:20 P.M.

"Can't sleep, baby?" That's what Mama says
when I find her in the kitchen late at night. She
is looking in her recipe book. Sam's birthday is
coming up, and she wants to bake a special
cake with frosting. "I don't like boys," I say,
"and especially Rudy. He was reading my private
things and now *he* won't talk to me!" Mama's
eyebrows go up when I tell her I said something
mean (and maybe it was very mean) to Rudy,
how it just came blubbering out of me. Mama
says being a friend is hard work sometimes.
I try to explain I'm NOT Rudy's friend, but
here comes a big speech: "Anyone can make
a mistake, Katie, but only a very big-hearted
person knows how to say, 'I'm sorry.'"

> Dear Rudy,
> You shouldn't go spying around,
> reading things that aren't your business.
> Signed, Katie Roberts

> Dear Rudy,
> You'd better come to the library on
> Tuesday. We're having a spelling test.
> You need practice.
> Signed, Katie your tutor

83

Dear Rudy,
Matthew can teach you how to play baseball. He knows a lot. If you want, I can ask Matthew (to help you). He has a dog.

From, Katie
P.S. In Rome, what do those kids do at recess? Any baseball?

Dear Rudy,
I'm sorry (about what I said).

Your friend Katie Roberts

Tomorrow I'll give my letter to Rudy before school. I hope no one sees.

March 16, 7:30 P.M.

Rudy came back to the library today. He had a good attitude.

March 17, 1949

Dear Mrs. Leitstein,

Something bad happened. A big truck hit my
mother on Main Street when she was crossing the
street. There was an ambulance, and what if
Mama dies? I'll be all alone like a poor orphan girl.

Sam isn't my father, don't forget. He'll keep
loving Billy and Seymour, but what about me?
Please, can I come and live with you? I'll be good
and I'll do a lot of chores and I won't be too moody
most of the time. I'm so scared, Mrs. Leitstein.
What should I do?

Love,

Katie

Katie

March 17, 9:30 P.M.

I HATE today and **I HATE** that truck and
that stupid truck driver. It's the worst day in the
world. We were bringing Mama's cake to the
café to surprise Sam for his birthday. Billy and
Seymour had balloons. Mama wore a new white
blouse and lipstick and pearls. She looked pretty
and Sam gave her a big kiss right there in front

of all those customers. Which he shouldn't have. Then Mama said, "Ooops! I left the surprise in the car," and she ran outside, and that's when that STUPID truck hit Mama. The ambulance had a red light.

Tonight Sam made dinner, and everything tasted terrible, and the babies were squishing peas and throwing peas as if everything were normal. I made Sam promise Mama won't die in that hospital. "Promise, Sam, promise. . . ." I kept saying that a million times. He said, "Your Mama's banged up and bruised, and a lot of her hurts, but it's not the kind of hurting that makes you die." "Promise and swear," I said. He promised and swore. And he'd better not lie.

Every single second I say a prayer: Mama, don't die. Mama, don't die.

March 18, 8:31 P.M.

Mean Sam made me go to school, but of course *he* got to go to the hospital. All I wanted was to be with Mama, but no one ever cares about me and my feelings. He's not my father—he can't tell me what to do! I was crying so much and screaming at Sam. The café was closed today. Marilyn's in *my* house taking care of *my* babies.

She thinks they like her but they don't. They only like me. And Mama.

At school, Miss Casey was extra nice. She didn't call on me in math, not even once. At lunchtime, the cafeteria was too noisy, and I ate in the classroom with Miss Casey. Lucie, too. She kept saying, "You're my only best friend forever," but I was thinking about Mama. Marilyn's jelly sandwich was bad. Or maybe I just wasn't hungry.

I made a get-well picture for Mama. Two adorable babies and a too-tall girl and a cow with a sign that says "We Love Mama." I wrote a letter to go with the picture.

Dear Mama,

Please come home. Nothing is the same when you're not around. I'm sorry I borrowed your lipstick without asking. I'm sorry I don't help around the house sometimes. Don't worry, because from now on, I'm going to help a lot. You'll see!

Love,

Katie
Katie, your daughter

At 3:00 Sam was waiting in front of school. We drove to the hospital. My stomach was churning the whole time and I kept saying, "Hurry, Sam, hurry," but he wouldn't drive fast. You're not allowed to run in a hospital, but I was running to room 100, and then I was kissing Mama. She smiled the teeniest little smile in the world and squeezed my hand, and when I whispered, "Please, don't die," she winked the eye that wasn't puffy. I ran out of the room to cry.

Poor Mama. Really, she's the best mother in the world. Starting today I'm going to be the best child in the world, just as long as she gets better. The hospital has a bad smell. I hate it there.

1 puffy eye
1 cut cheek
4 broken ribs
2 black-and-blue arms
1 broken leg

I'm supposed to be doing homework, but it's lonely in the kitchen and I'm not in the mood. Sam is playing with Billy and Seymour on the living room floor, even though it's way past their bedtime. Seymour was looking behind the couch calling, "Mama Mama." Then Billy started to cry. They miss Mama, but I miss her more. I keep asking Sam, "When is she coming home, when, when, when?" The doctor says a week, or maybe more. Too long! I want my mother. Home! Now!

March 22, 5:10 P.M.

Message to Notebook from Katie, Who Is Hiding in Her Tree House, Where No One Can Find Her and Make Her Do More Work!

I'm doing millions and millions of things in this house and no one ever says thank you. Dishes. Peel potatoes. Babies. Squeeze oranges for juice. Babies. Laundry to put in the wash. Babies. Laundry to hang on the line. Babies. Laundry to fold. Babies. Laundry to put away. Dishes to wash. Dishes to dry. Dishes to put away. Tomatoes to slice for the salad. Babies, they want you every second. And that Marilyn thinks she's the boss of me, ha! Her spaghetti sauce isn't good like Mama's. Maybe I'll just eat cookies in my tree house for dinner. Too bad, Marilyn.

I made a new picture for Mama. Flowers in a basket, and inside the basket there's a poem.

March 26, 4:30 P.M.

We were playing volleyball in gym and I kept serving into the net and the whole world was laughing, and I started to cry. Then Lucie was yelling, "You're the meanest kids in Texas. Don't you know her mother's in the hospital!" Miss Rogers let Lucie and me sit in her office a while. There's a water fountain there, and magazines. Rudy came in, and Matthew. Joyce, too, with caramels in her pocket, and she gave us each a caramel, and it was sticking in our teeth. They were trying to cheer me up. Which was nice of them.

March 30, 10:22 P.M.

GREAT DAY! BEST DAY!
BEST DAY IN THE WORLD!

Mama came home from the hospital! Sam parked the car and carried her up the porch steps. I was jumping up and down, holding her hand and kissing it 2000 times. Billy and Seymour kept looking at Mama, but wouldn't come close, and she said, "Sweeties, it's me, don't you know your own mama, with this funny old leg in a cast?" It was sad, you knew she wanted to hug those babies so much. Then Sam said,

"There's someone in the car who wants to see you, Katie," and guess who was sitting in the back seat. MRS. LEITSTEIN! What a big surprise, and it's all because of my letter! Because when it came in the mail, she said to herself, "Well, Mrs. Leitstein, looks like you're needed in Texas." She packed her suitcases fast. Then took a train all the way to Texas.

In the afternoon, Mama was resting on a chair in the yard, and I was showing Mrs. Leitstein all around the ranch. She kept saying, "What a grand house, Katie," and she was wearing the apron I made. I begged and begged and finally Sam and Mr. Trimmer moved the guest bed into my room. Now Mrs. L and I can be roommates! We'll talk all night and Mama won't know!

We had company: Mr. Pergolizzi. He brought flowers for Mama. Rudy came too. And Matthew's mother. She made apple pie, and I had *two* pieces with ice cream! Matthew came, too, and his baby sister, Jamie. Matthew and Rudy were playing catch in the yard and they forgot to ask me. Boy, are they rude.

"It was very charming to meet you," that's what Mr. Pergolizzi said to Mrs. Leitstein when he was going home. Charming! I like that word. When I grow up and write books, I'm going to use it a lot. The people in my books will all be charming, ha!

April 2, 5:07 P.M.

I keep trying to teach Billy and Seymour how to walk; they're getting too heavy to carry. They love to crawl fast. They even crawl backwards, and stand without holding on. They jump holding on, and roll down the hill in the yard. But they just won't walk. Walk, babies, walk!

I wish Mama could walk. Her leg is taking too long to get better. She's sick and tired of sitting around all day. She says it makes her cranky and it does. A hundred times she gets in a bad bossy mood, saying, "Do this, Katie, do that, Katie." I get mad. But then you look at the big heavy cast on Mama's leg, and you feel bad.

9:00 P.M.

NEWS FLASH, Whoa!

Mrs. Leitstein's at the movies! With Mr. Pergolizzi! Poor Mrs. L, she couldn't decide what to wear. She kept saying, "I'm frazzled! I'm frazzled!" Mama was propped up in her bed, and we were bringing in this dress and that dress and Mama shook her head. . . . "Too fancy for a first date . . . Too plain . . . Too pale."

Finally, navy blue was the winner, and I gave Mrs. L my favorite red sweater for good luck. Aren't I charming! Well, I hope Mrs. Leitstein likes the movie and I hope she isn't frazzled. I'm going to stay up until she gets home (even if it's midnight) so she can tell me all about it.

April 18, 6:00 P.M.

When I got home from school, the kitchen smelled sooo good. Well, Mrs. Leitstein was cooking up a storm for Passover. Mama was helping, but you could tell her ribs hurt when she moved around too much. Mrs. L kept telling Mama, "Go sit down. Go sit down." It was fun watching someone boss Mama for a change! There was a big pot of matzo ball soup on the stove, and I kept eating from the pot with the big ladle, saying, "More, more, more!"

Mrs. Leitstein and I set the table. We used the good china and Mama's favorite tablecloth. It's pretty white lace, and a long time ago it was her mother's. Mama said not to forget to set two extra places, for Rudy and Mr. Pergolizzi. "That's not fair!" I yelled, "No boys for dinner!" Mama made a big giant speech, of course. "For once step out of yourself, Katie." "You are not the center of the universe, Katie." "Passover is family time, Katie." "Imagine Rudy and Mr. Pergolizzi all by themselves on the holiday. . . ."

I called Lucie to complain, but she said I was lucky. The only boys who come to her house for dinner are her brothers, and she's tired of them. Then we were deciding what I should wear, and this is what we decided: Navy blue skirt (pleats). White blouse (red trim on collar, and it's my favorite blouse in the world). No socks. I hope everyone thinks I look pretty.

Big News of the Century

Mama said I can wear lipstick—it's about time! Happy Passover, from Miss Beautiful Lips.

April 21, 4:30 P.M.

Miss Casey fired me, and I am mad at Miss Casey. *She* said Rudy doesn't need a spelling tutor anymore. *I* said he still spells lots of words wrong. Then *she* said spelling tests don't lie, and that was the end of that. As a special treat for all my hard work, I'm allowed to read to 1st graders two times next week.

Secret : I wish I could still be Rudy's tutor, because I like walking around with my folder. Everyone knows there are important papers in there. And also because . . . very big secret . . . shhh . . . I think I like Rudy! More than David, ha, and this is why I like Rudy . . . shhh. . . .

1. *Cute.* Definitely, especially when he gets a haircut and his hair's all curly and cute.

2. *Good Artist.* Today in art Rudy was painting a house and he told me it was his house in Italy. There were stairs and they looked so real, and all of a sudden, I was thinking about other stairs, winding stairs in my old apartment house in NY City. I made a picture. Rudy said, "How come you don't put people on those stairs?" So I put three people there. Me. Mama. And my father in his soldier clothes. Going-to-war clothes. I liked my picture but it made me sad.

3. *Has a really nice grampa.* Mr. Pergolizzi calls Mrs. Leitstein every night! At exactly 6:30! Whenever the phone rings at 6:30, Mrs. L pretends not to hear. Her cheeks get pink and she starts to clear the table. Mama looks at Sam. Sam looks at Mama. Billy and Seymour go, "R-r-r-i-i-i-n-g-g." I get the phone, and it's always Mr. Pergolizzi. He gave a whole big box of chocolates to Mrs. Leitstein! We each have two when we are talking in our beds at night and the lights are off. Shhh. Don't say a word to Mama.

4. Knows how to use a cash register.

I told Lucie about liking Rudy. She swore not to tell a soul. Especially Joyce. Lucie told me a secret, too. Last month she wrote another letter to Leo in Houston. He didn't write back. That makes two times he didn't write back. Lucie says if he ever does (write), she's throwing his letter in the garbage. If I ever get a letter from a boy, I'm not throwing it in the garbage!

April 23, 1:30 P.M.

Happy Birthday to you
Happy Birthday to you
Happy Birthday,
Dear Billy and Seymour,
Happy Birthday to you!

May 1, 8:30 A.M.

We were making the bed and Mrs. Leitstein told
me a secret. She likes Mr. Pergolizzi! He likes her,
too! What a great secret! The only person I'm
telling is Lucie. And Mama. She needs cheering
up. Boy, she hates that broken leg! Because it
hurts when she tries to walk and because she
hates when everyone is waiting on her all the
time. I wish people were waiting on me. I wish I
had a servant. When I grow up, I want lots of
servants. The first thing they'll do is bring me
breakfast in bed. Pancakes and chocolate milk.
Every single morning.

Look, look! Billy took four steps! All by
himself and I wasn't holding his fingers!
When Seymour saw that, he slid off Mama's
lap. I held out my hands and he took one
teeny step. Then he took a too-big step
and lost his balance, and I scooped him
right up. We were all clapping like
crazy. Go, Billy! And Seymour!

Go Billy!
Go Seymour!

May 7, 6:00 P.M.

The BABIES in this house are terrible, horrible,
poem-eating brats! This is what happened. I was
sitting on the floor in the kitchen, working so

hard on my poem, and it had feeling, and Miss
Casey was finally going to like it, and the phone
was ringing, and it was Lucie. Big news, Lucie
got a letter! From Leo! She was screaming into
the telephone and I could hear her jumping up
and down. She read me the letter. Three times.

Dear Lucie,
How are you? I am fine. Romper, my dog, ran out
in the road and nearly got run down, but he's okay.
They put a bandage on his eye.

From, Leo

I was wishing some boy wrote that letter to
me. Then! Suddenly! Billy was stealing my poem
and ripping it and putting it in his mouth! I was
yelling and mad. Well, Mama scooped up Billy,
and he kept crying, crying, crying. What a faker,
I didn't do anything to him! He's the one who
ate *my* poem that I've been working on for such
a long time. I kept explaining that to Mama and
I was crying, too, but of course she didn't care
about *me.* She only cared about that bad baby
and she was rocking him like he was the only
child in the room, and he was all hot and
hiccuppy like the big drama star that he is. Then
Seymour was crying for no reason at all, and that
made two bad babies. Which is just what I told
Mama, and she said, "Go to your room, young

my poem

lady, until you calm down." Which is where I am right now and I'll never come out again. Even if she's making the best thing in the world for dinner, like macaroni. I'll just sit here starving away; she'll be sorry.

May 7, 8:15 P.M.

Mama pasted torn-up paper like a puzzle. When all the pieces were together, she read my poem. Two times. Then she gave me a big hug. Mama likes my poem! She says it has heart.

My House, by Katie Roberts

I miss my house.
We had winding stairs
and you could see the river

Then the war came, and my
father packed his duffel.

We had winding stairs
and you could see the river
I wish my father came home
from the war.

I might take my poem to school tomorrow for a surprise for Miss Casey. Or I might hang it in my room. Over my desk where I can see it all the time.

Now hear this! Mr. Pergolizzi wants to get married! To Mrs. Leitstein! She told us when we were having dinner, before dessert, and what a big surprise. "Mama and Sam and I were clapping and going, "Yeaaaaa," and I was saying, "Can I be the bridesmaid, please, please, please?" But poor Mrs. L, she was too confused.

Confusion # 1. Isn't she too old to be a bride?

Confusion # 2. How will she get used to living in Texas?

Confusion # 3. What about Mr. Leitstein? Because she still loves him so much, even though he died a long time ago.

Mama gave her a giant hug. She said, "You're getting a second chance at love, Mrs. Leitstein, and isn't that nice, because I got a second chance, too!" Then Mama winked at Sam. One of those winks that means "I love you," and it's sooo annoying. I was thinking and thinking and trying to remember something Mrs. Leitstein once told me before we moved to Texas, when I was so scared. Then I remembered. "Love is risky," I said in a big voice, "but it's worth it."

Everyone looked at me. They didn't say a word.
I guess they were thinking how mature I am.

Will Mrs. Leitstein marry Mr. Pergolizzi?

Yes. No. YES. No. Yes. No. YES.

May 14, 6:15 P.M.

The Wedding Poem, by Katie Roberts, child poet:

Yo ho ho
Katie gets to go
to a wedding
Yo ho ho

Guess what, Mama said I can invite Lucie to
the wedding! This is a very lucky thing, because
it turns out Rudy invited Matthew, and it would
be totally 100% not fair if Rudy got to have a
friend and I didn't. Lucie and I were talking
all about the wedding at lunch and drawing
pictures of wedding gowns. Joyce was mad, you
could tell. She was pretending to be best friends
with Pamela. Well, fine with me because I like
having Lucie all to myself. So there to you, Joyce!

This is sad. I stayed after school to wash the

blackboards, which is so much fun because you get to be alone with Miss Casey, and her shoes are under the desk, not on her feet, and she gives you cookies. I was washing with the yellow sponge, telling Miss Casey all about the wedding, then all of a sudden, she was crying into a hankie. I got scared because I'd never seen a teacher cry before. Then she told me a secret, that a long time ago she loved a boy, they were even engaged, that's how in love they were, but he died in the war. When I heard that, I wanted to hug my teacher the way Mama hugs me when I feel bad. I told Miss Casey I think she's the prettiest teacher in the world, and also the nicest. Then I went back to washing the blackboard.

May 16, 5:30 A.M.

When I Grow Up, Here's What's Going to Happen.

1. I will be a famous writer of important books, and sometimes I'll be a newspaper person. And a waitress at the Trolley Car Café.

$2.$ I will travel all around the world, whenever I want. My favorite place is New York City, of course, and I will go there often. Especially the Empire State Building. When I go to Paris, I will visit the Eiffel Tower. I will speak French, and wear a black beret.

$3.$ I will go to millions of parties, and handsome boys will dance with me until my feet fall off. If a boy named David asks me to dance, I will say, "No, thank you, I don't care for you one bit." I will wear long dresses that look like gowns, and a lot of them are black. My hair will be long, too.

May 19, 11:00 A.M.

Hey, Notebook, here I am, it's me, Katie Roberts, way up high in my tree house, and in one more hour, I'm going to a wedding! Rudy's here, too, talking too much and blabbing away about his hero Jackie Robinson. The ceremony will be in the yard. We have a special canopy there. Which is where you stand at a wedding when everyone is Jewish. The rabbi's in the kitchen, talking to the grownups. He's the same one who married Mama and Sam, but the people who are getting married today are . . . ta daaa! . . . Mrs. Leitstein and Mr. Pergolizzi. I am very excited, and my dress is blue, and there's a matching jacket with red buttons. Guess what, my shoes have heels! Sam said,

"We're never going to be millionaires, but things are picking up at the Trolley Car Café, so how about new shoes for the wedding, Katie?" He drove me to the shoe store and I showed him my favorite reds, and we bought them. But then I was scared the whole way home about Mama being mad. Which she wasn't. Which is a lucky thing, because I love my shoes so much. Except, they sometimes make you trip. No one ever told me you have to walk like a grown-up lady when you wear high heels. It spoils everything. There's a little gold ring in my pocket for Mrs. Leitstein. Which I get to give her during the ceremony. Important job. Rudy has another ring in his pocket, for his grampa. Rudy likes Mrs. Leitstein, she reminds him of his grandma.

Well, I'm all mixed-up, happy and sad. Because I love when Mrs. Leitstein's in the bed across the room in the morning, and I love when she's here after school, and I wish she could stay forever. It's not fair Rudy gets her all the time. She's mine. Mama says Rudy needs Mrs. Leitstein. *I* need her. Mama says Mrs. L has plenty of love to go around, and I can visit the apartment over the sewing shop anytime I want, but it's not the same as having her here. Her wedding dress is pink, and she's wearing Mama's pearls but no high heels. I love Mrs. Leitstein.

I am looking at my father's watch, thinking, "Hello Daddy, it's me, your little girl, Katie, and look at me with heels! Mama's better now, and her leg is nearly fixed, but the cut on her cheek left a scar. Don't worry, because she's still really pretty. Even though her hair's too short. I wish you were here with us in Texas, Daddy. I'd give you the biggest slice of wedding cake, and the biggest kiss hello. . . ."

Today is a very nice day in Texas. The sky is blue and the clouds are puffy and white and moving fast. Billy and Seymour are walking and running and pushing toys across the yard. They better not make noise at the wedding! Uh-oh, here come Sam and Mama . . . across the yard, down the sloping hill . . . and Mama's calling, "Katie, come down from that tree house. Put your shoes on *now*. We're going to a wedding!"

Praise for Katie Roberts

★ "Keenly—and humorously—aware of the injustices that have been flung upon her, this fresh character will win readers as she surmounts hurdle after hurdle."
—*Publishers Weekly* (starred review)

★ "Katie is a captivating, outspoken protagonist whose concerns will be familiar to many children, and Hest's satisfying, realistic conclusion leaves the girl sure of her place in her new, blended family."
—*Booklist* (starred review)

"Like Beverly Cleary, [Amy Hest] understands and respects her readers. . . . A finely crafted story." —*The Horn Book*

"A rollicking story that balances humor and pre-adolescent angst with the larger canvas of post-WWII America." —*Kirkus Reviews*

"With believable characters and a touch of romance, Hest's book should prove popular."
—*School Library Journal*

AMY HEST lives in Katie Roberts's hometown of New York City. She is the author of many books for children, including the picture books *Kiss Good Night*, illustrated by Anita Jeram; *When Jessie Came Across the Sea*, illustrated by P.J. Lynch; and the Baby Duck books, illustrated by Jill Barton. She is also the author of another novel about Katie Roberts, *Love You, Soldier*.

⚜ ☙ ⚜

The stories in this collection were previously published individually by Candlewick Press.

The Private Notebook of Katie Roberts, age 11 text © 1995 by Amy Hest
The Private Notebook of Katie Roberts, age 11 illustrations © 1995 by Sonja Lamut
The Great Green Notebook of Katie Roberts: who just turned 12 on Monday
text © 1998 by Amy Hest
The Great Green Notebook of Katie Roberts: who just turned 12 on Monday
illustrations © 1998 by Sonja Lamut

First edition in this format 2005

The Library of Congress has cataloged the hardcover editions as follows:

Hest, Amy.
The private notebook of Katie Roberts, age 11/Amy Hest ; illustrated by Sonja Lamut.—1st ed.
p. cm.
Summary: In a series of journal entries and letters to a pen pal, Katie
relates her feelings about her father's death in World War II, her mother's remarriage,
and the family's move from New York City to Texas.
ISBN 1-56402-474-1 (hardcover)
[1. Moving, Household—Fiction. 2. Remarriage—Fiction. 3. Diaries—Fiction.
4. Jews—United States—Fiction. 5. Texas—Fiction.]
I. Lamut, Sonja, ill. II. Title.
PZ7.H4375Pr 1995 94-37737
[Fic] — dc20

Hest, Amy.
The Great Green Notebook of Katie Roberts:
who just turned 12 on Monday/Amy Hest; illustrated by Sonja Lamut. 1st ed.
p. cm.
Summary: In a series of journal entries, letters, pictures, and drawings,
Katie relates her feelings about her mother, baby brothers, new friends,
school, boys, the Italian immigrant she tutors, and growing up.
ISBN 0-7636-0464-X (hardcover)
[1. Family life—Fiction. 2. Schools—Fiction. 3. Diaries—Fiction.]
I. Lamut, Sonja, ill. II. Title.
PZ7.H4375G 1998 98-16839
[Fic]—DC21

ISBN 0-7636-2698-8 (hardcover collection)

2 4 6 8 10 9 7 5 3 1

Printed in the United States of America

This book was typeset in Berkeley Old Style and Myriad.

Candlewick Press
2067 Masachusetts Avenue
Cambridge, Massachusetts 02140

visit us at www.candlewick.com